ALPHA SECURITY

THE COMPLETE ROMANCE SERIES

HOPE FORD

PROTECTING HER

1

SIERRA

Running into Knox Tavern, I'm out of breath and out of patience. I'm here to find my late brother's best friend. My brother died while he was serving in the army. He stepped on a bomb and was gone from us forever. He and his best friend, Johnny, had joined together and it's been one year since my brother died and Johnny's life fell apart. He was also hurt in the explosion and was honorably discharged. He hasn't been the same since and sometimes I think he wishes he too had died.

I've tried to help him, but I'm worn out now. First, little things were missing from my house. Today, my laptop and television were taken and before I call the police I'm going to get it back from Johnny. I've tried to help him. My brother would want me to help him, but I know he wouldn't want me to put up with this.

And in all honestly, I know it's not Johnny doing this. It's the drugs that have got a hold of him and dragged him down into this abyss he can't crawl out of. If he was himself, he would never do this. He would never hurt me like he has.

Looking around, I approach a waiter carrying a tray to the table. "Hey, is Johnny here?"

He throws his finger up and points to the back of the restaurant. I start walking in that direction and a tall, good-looking man walks out through the kitchen door.

"Hello. Can you tell me if Johnny is working?" I ask him.

He looks at me with distrust in his eyes. "He no longer works here."

Exasperated at this point, I now know why he ripped me off. If he was fired, he's not bringing in tips. No tips means no money and no money means no drugs. If only I can convince him to go to rehab. "What did he do this time?"

"You know I can't tell you that." He starts to walk away from me.

"Are you the owner?" When he merely nods at me, I

say, "Please, don't call the police. He has a problem and I'm just trying to help him. Did he take money?"

"How did you know that?" he asks me suspiciously, like I had something to do with it.

Putting my hands up in front of me, I explain, "He was my brother's best friend and they served in the army together. They were both hurt from a bomb but my brother didn't make it. Johnny is all I have left of him. He got mixed up with drugs and I'm just trying to help him. He stole from me this morning while I was in class. That's why I'm looking for him."

He looks at me and I hope he sees the sincerity in my face. "You shouldn't be mixed up with him. It's only going to get worse. He has to want help."

Defiantly, I snap back at him. "You think I don't know that? I do. Look, can I just pay you what he owes you and you leave the cops out of it?"

He stares back at me for a minute and then tells me to wait here, he'll be right back.

When he returns, he has a large man with him. They are both tall, but his friend towers over him. He has on a black T-shirt and black pants. He has tattoos down his arms and his shirt has a logo on it that says Alpha Security. His muscle under the logo twitches at my scrutiny. My eyes fly up to his and he's looking at me so intensely I can't look away.

"I'm sorry, I didn't get your name," the owner asks me.

Blinking, I break the connection with Alpha Security guy and look back at the owner of the restaurant. "Sierra," I say and try to train my eyes on him instead.

"Sierra, I'm Brody. And this is Ryder, one of the owners of Alpha Security. He is here changing locks and updating our security since we had some money and keys stolen."

I can't stop myself from cringing and thinking, *Oh, Johnny, what have you gotten yourself into now?*

He continues, "I am not going to press charges on your friend. However, if he comes in here again, my decision will change."

I thank him appreciatively, but my eyes keep straying over to Ryder and I see him watching me intently.

"However, there is a catch..." Brody adds.

Instantly, I back up and look between them. "I brought Ryder out here because I think you need to talk to him about a security system. I know you are trying to help a friend, but I'm afraid this may get worse."

I look over at Ryder and his face is drawn tight. He still hasn't said a word.

"I really don't think I need a security..."

Brody interrupts me. "He broke into your house and stole from you... I think you do."

Shrugging my shoulders in defeat, I give in. Honestly, it's probably not a bad idea. "I will call them when I get paid this Friday."

"No. I'm going to set it up today." Ryder hasn't said a word until now, and I feel chills slide down my arms at the sound of his voice. It's deep and scratchy, like he doesn't talk much, but when he does he gets his point across.

He's looking straight at me and I almost shy away from his look but I stop myself. "I don't get paid until Friday."

He doesn't respond to me. He tells Brody that he has everything set up in the back and drops a set of keys on the counter for him. "Here's all your keys. Call me if you need anything else."

They must be friends. Ryder is almost dismissing

Brody and all Brody does is look between the two of us and nod as he walks away. I remember at the last minute to holler out *Thank you* to him.

When we are left alone just starting at each other, I ask Ryder, "Uh, do you have a card so I can call you, uh, Friday?"

Ryder

WHEN I WALKED out from the back of Knox Tavern, I expected to meet a future client. Brody didn't give me any details, except a woman out front needed her house secured. But the moment I saw her, I knew I would make sure she was protected. I stood here, silently listening to her and Brody talk about her "friend." While they were talking, I couldn't take my eyes off her. She has long brown hair that is pulled back in a ponytail. She has on short jean shorts, showing off her thick thighs. Her T-shirt is stretched tightly across her large breasts and I can't help but appreciate every curve she has. From this angle, I can see the slope of her ass and my mouth waters.

Being this close to her, I realize how short she really

is. She's tiny compared to me and that makes me even more protective.

"I'm free this afternoon. I would like to go ahead and do it today," I tell her.

"But how much is it?" she asks me, still not budging.

I decide right then to take control of the situation. Grabbing her hand with mine, I appreciate the feel of her smaller one in my larger one before tugging her toward the door. "Today I will just do an estimate. Tell you what you need. We can discuss prices and everything once I know exactly what you need. Where's your car?"

"I don't have one. I just take the bus," she tells me and I hold her hand a little tighter. Hell. The image of her sweetness riding on a public bus bothers me. Irritates me more than I would have thought.

I lead her over to my truck. "Okay, we will go in my truck then. Hop in." I pull open the door and she pulls her hand from mine.

"I really can't pay you until Friday. And I want to be honest with you, if it's going to be more than $100, I will have to wait longer."

She's embarrassed and I don't want that. I don't ever

want her to feel embarrassed with me. "I'm not worried about it, Sierra. I promise."

She reluctantly climbs into my truck and I resist gripping onto her hips and putting her into the seat. I'm already a possessive pushy asshole, I don't want to scare her off.

Once I'm settled in the driver's seat, she tells me where to go. I ask her what happened for her to need a security system.

She takes a deep breath and finally admits, "A friend of mine has gotten mixed up with drugs and he stole a few things from me."

My hands tighten on the steering wheel. "Drugs make people do crazy things, honey. But you deserve better than a boyfriend that would do this to you."

She starts laughing. "Boyfriend? He's not my boyfriend." And then she tells me the story of her brother and his best friend. I can't help but feel bad for her knowing she feels like she is torn between doing what is best for her but also trying to help her brother's best friend. I'm relieved that I'm not dealing with a boyfriend, but it still bothers me that she trusts this man so much.

"And you thought you would just come to the

restaurant and face him down... get your money back?"

She shrugs her shoulders. "He won't hurt me. He's just messed up right now."

I want to tell her exactly how dangerous he could be. I don't know what drugs he is on, but I'm assuming he's digging himself deeper if he is stealing from his job and from Sierra.

When we pull up to her apartment, I walk around to open her door and take in the area. She lives in a rougher part of town, but until I can figure out the situation better, I am going to have to protect her here.

Her face is red and I ask her about it only to have her flush deeper.

"This is ridiculous. Your truck is probably worth more than everything I have in my apartment. It's crazy to get a security system for my stuff. I don't have anything of value... especially now."

She walks ahead of me and I keep my eyes trained on the back of her head. She doesn't need me ogling her ass when she is feeling so vulnerable.

When she opens her door, I stop her before she

walks in. I put my hands on each of her shoulders and she tips her head back to look at me.

"The security is for you, Sierra. To protect you."

"But he won't…"

I stop her before she can even finish the sentence. "We don't know that. We don't know what he's capable of right now. Until we do, I'll feel better knowing you are protected."

The stress is evident on her face and I can tell she's not used to having someone take care of her. She looks up at me with confusion in her expression. "Why are you doing this? Why do you care?"

Without any hesitation, I tell her, "When I saw you today I knew that I had to protect you. I won't rest unless I know you are okay. I don't really understand it, but I know I have to make sure you are okay."

She considers my answer for a minute and then just nods her head. When I slide my hand down her shoulders and trail along the cold chills on her arms, I wonder if she is feeling anything for me.

Walking into her living room, I glance around briefly. I already know I need to work on lighting the parking lot, and her front door more. She has one simple lock on her front door and as I inspect the windows, some of them are even unlocked. I figure she doesn't need me admonishing her right now, so I just go through the house securing the rest of the windows. She sits on the couch while I do the walk-through. When I go into her bedroom, the scent of lavender and vanilla hits me and I now associate that smell with her. I try not to look at the bed with its rumpled blankets and pillow with the indention from her head on it.

After evaluating everything, I don't wait; I get started. The lighting will have to wait until tomorrow, but locks and alarms I can do now.

"I thought you were only doing an estimate?" She interrupts my thoughts by walking into the bedroom.

2

SIERRA

When I walk into my bedroom and see him on his knees securing something to my window, I stop and watch him. Just the thought that he is in my bedroom makes my lower belly quiver. He's so handsome, and so possessive… even though he has no reason to be.

"I thought you were only doing an estimate?" I ask him.

He doesn't stop working. "I'm going to go ahead and secure all your windows, especially since you are on the first floor. And take care of your door."

"But how much is this going to cost?" I know I'm getting frustrated with him and he's only trying to help. But I can't afford to pay a lot.

"Quit worrying about it, Sierra." He pulls his wallet

out of the back of his pants and hands me his credit card. "Hey, will you order some food for us? I'm starving."

"You are not buying food. I'll fix us something." I hand him back the card and walk out of the room. I can't let him buy me food, I'm already going to owe him so much money as it is.

I walk into the kitchen and look to see what I have. I have all the fixin's for spaghetti except the hamburger. I shrug. Oh well, it's better than nothing.

As I start cooking, he goes room to room and is done by the time the food is ready. When he walks into the kitchen, I tell him, "I hope spaghetti is okay. I didn't have any hamburger, so it's just marinara sauce." And I pray that my face doesn't go red again.

He doesn't bat an eye. "It smells great!"

He washes his hands at my dingy sink and I know that he is totally out of his element here. My parents have been gone since I was in high school. My brother was all I had left in this world and when he died, I really struggled to keep moving. I was able to get a full scholarship, but it didn't include housing. My apartment is cheaper than the dorms and I make enough at my waitressing job to pay for rent and food. But after that, there's not much money left.

I sit down at the table with the mismatched chairs. I raise my head, determined to not feel so insecure in my own home. I work hard for this and really have no reason to be ashamed.

I dish him out a plate and he digs in heartily. He makes all the sounds that he is enjoying his food and I can't help but smile over at him.

We talk and he tells me about his twenty years in the army. It makes me wonder if he's helping me because of the army brotherhood, but then I remember he didn't know about my brother until we were on the way to my apartment. Maybe he is just one of those men that wants to save a damsel in distress.

I find out he's 42, 22 years older than me. He didn't bat an eye when I told him my age.

"So what all did he steal?" he asks me as he helps clean up the dishes, even after I insisted I could do them on my own.

"Uh, this time?... my laptop and my television."

He doesn't comment, just nods at me. I am going to be spending a lot of time at the library now to use their computers. Maybe I can find one at a pawn shop in the next few weeks.

After dinner, Ryder gathers up all his stuff and I walk him to the door. He shows me how to set the alarm and makes me promise to arm it, even when I'm in the house. He programs his number into my phone and calls himself so he has my number.

I tell him I will bring him money this Friday and all he does is bends down and kisses me on the forehead before walking out the door, with another reminder to set the alarm.

Ryder

IT WAS hard to leave her, but I knew I had to. I wanted to stay, even if I just held her all night. And truthfully, that scared the fuck out of me. I've had relationships in the past, but I've never felt this instant pull toward someone. I want to protect her, to possess her and claim her.

Walking out of her apartment, I noted some more things that needed to be worked on. I called Charlie, one of my associates, and had her come and wait outside the apartment so I could go shopping, go home and shower. I trust the security system I installed, but I don't know exactly what I'm dealing with here. Until the intel on Johnny comes back, I plan on keeping an eye on Sierra.

I stopped by an electronics store and got Sierra a new computer. I wasn't sure what all software she needed, so I had them install what most college students use. Then I went home and after taking a quick shower, I drove back to Sierra's. Charlie waved at me as she pulled away and I took her spot. I lie back in my seat and watch the building.

Around eight in the morning, Sierra walks out of her apartment. She's wearing a black skirt that is a little too short for my liking. Don't get me wrong, she looks hot, but I don't want others to see her in it. Her white button-up has the top two buttons undone and even from this far, I can see her cleavage on display. What the fuck? I groan and adjust my cock in my pants.

I jump out of my truck and at the slam of the door she looks my way. "Ryder, uh, what are you doing here?"

"You said you had to be at work early this morning, so I came to take you." I grab her hand and pull her against me. The scent of lavender and honey fills my nostrils and I inhale deeply, wanting to commit it to memory.

"You've already done so much, you didn't have to do that," she admonishes me. "I could have just taken the bus."

"I wanted to. Plus, I got you something." Opening the door, I help her up into the truck. This time, I do it, I put my hands around her thick waist and lift her up into the cab of my truck. When I get in, I reach into the back seat and lift the bag up to put in her lap.

She smiles at me and looks so excited as she opens the bag. Her mouth drops open as she pulls out the laptop. "It's a computer. And not just any computer. This is top of the line, Ryder. I know this probably cost you two thousand dollars. I can't accept this."

She starts to put it back into the bag, but I put my hand out and stop her.

"It's not a big deal, honey. You needed a computer for school," I try to reason with her.

"Yeah, but I planned to get one from the pawn shop or something. It will take me forever to pay you back," she says, deflated now when she was so happy a few minutes ago.

It kills me that she would have been happy with a computer from the pawn shop. She has already proven to me that she is not vain or materialistic and she works hard for everything she has. It makes me want to give her everything she wants or needs.

"You are not paying me back. I wanted to do this for you. Just accept it and say thank you. Please. It's a gift. You can't say no without hurting my feelings." I give her my most innocent look.

She hesitates even longer, looking between the bag and me until finally she gives in. "Okay. Thank you, Ryder. I do appreciate this. And everything else you've done for me." She leans over the console to kiss me on the cheek. I stop her from pulling back and bring her lips to mine. I wanted to give her time to get used to me, but I can't resist kissing her when she's this close to me. Her lips open softly under the pressure of mine, but I refrain from deepening the kiss. I have no control when it comes to Sierra. She had me hooked even before this kiss.

As I pull back from her, her eyes are closed and she sticks her tongue out and swipes it along her lower lip. I brush a hair away from her face and hold her cheek in my hand. When she opens her eyes, we sit there looking at one another.

My face is in a full grin and with her brown eyes looking back at me, I lean in one more time to kiss her. Even with that brief touch of our lips, I want more.

Pulling back, I lean over and buckle her seat belt for her. Then, kissing her on the nose, I go back to my seat and take off toward her work. When I drop her off, I let her out of the truck, give her a quick kiss and make her promise me she will call me if she sees Johnny.

3

SIERRA

I worked all morning and then walked to class. Campus is less than a mile from my work. Sitting through a whole class of statistics makes my mind wander to Ryder. He's almost too good to be true. Just thinking about him makes me slide my legs together to feel the friction. I know my panties are wet and they have been since I met him yesterday. Yesterday! That's crazy I only met him twenty-four hours ago.

My phone vibrates in the pocket of my skirt. I look up at the professor and he is still going on and on about math. I pull my phone out and can't stop the smile from forming on my lips. It's Ryder.

Will you go out with me tonight?

My heart starts pounding in my chest; I swear I can see the movement in my shirt. I know I just met him, but I feel like I can trust him.

Yes, I type and push send before I second-guess myself.

The little bubble shows up telling me he is typing me back. *What time do you get out of class?*

I look up at the professor and he is still writing problems down on the board. *In 30 minutes. I will be home in an hour.*

I will pick you up from class. See you soon.

After class, I walk out of the math building and straight into a strong pair of arms that wrap around me. He kisses me briefly on the head, then tugs me toward his truck. I can see some women from my class eyeing me, and I can't help but beam proudly at having Ryder by my side.

He helps me into the truck. Once he's in and takes off down the road, I ask him, "Do I need to go home and change?"

Looking down at my bare legs, he grasps the console between us, like he's stopping himself from touching me. I still have on my black skirt, and it has now ridden up my thighs. I've removed my button-down and just have a white T-shirt on.

"You look perfect, Sierra." He grabs my hand and laces his fingers with mine.

He pulls into a new steakhouse. I've heard it's really good, but I haven't eaten here before. I would never been able to afford it.

Once we are seated and have ordered, he holds my hand. He had me sit next to him in the booth, instead of across from him, only telling me that he liked having me close.

We eat and laugh. He tells me about his company and I tell him about my parents, my brother and that I'm studying accounting in school.

Other than when he cuts his steak, he keeps his hand on my thigh through the whole meal. I shift in the seat a little, just to feel his hand tighten on my leg.

Dinner ends too quickly and before I know it we are on our way to my house.

When he takes me home, he walks me to my apartment.

"My goodness, the parking lot is lit up like Fort

Knox," I say in awe, looking at all the lights. "Did you do this?"

"Yes. I told you I was going to make sure you are safe." He unlocks my door and disarms the alarm for me, then walks through the small rooms just to double-check everything.

"Have you heard anything from Johnny?" he asks me when he walks back into the living room.

"No. Nothing. But I would say I won't hear from him for a week or two. He won't come around until he thinks I'm not mad anymore." I shrug.

"You know you can't keep letting him do this to you, honey. I won't let him hurt you again." He stands right in front of me and pulls my ponytail to force my head backwards to look up at him.

"I'm not going to let him. Not again." I smile at him. I should be mad that he's so controlling but all I feel when he gets like this is a slow burn that fills my body. He leans down and kisses me briefly with his hands gripping my hips. He pulls away from me and with one last glance, he leaves.

Ryder

THE NIGHT ENDS way too soon. I would have liked to take her to her bedroom or better yet, to my house, and keep her in bed with me.

But after I took her home and went through her apartment, I kissed her briefly on the lips with a promise to see her the next day. I know she's not ready for more.

Now I'm sitting in my truck outside of her apartment. I should just tell her what I'm doing but I don't want to scare her or anything. Truthfully, she's safe. I know she is safe. The lights and the alarm system should deter Johnny from coming back, but I'm not taking any chances. That's why I've arranged for Charlie or me to watch her most of the time.

My phone dings and I figure it's a text about work. I've had to hire some more installers because business is picking up. But it's not, it's a text from Sierra.

Thank you for tonight. I had a really good time.

A smile automatically forms on my lips. *Me too, honey. I didn't want to leave you.*

Her reply is almost instant. *Then why did you?*

I want to make sure you're ready. And when you are, I'll be waiting. There's no rush.

I stare at my phone. I can see she read my text, but there is no response. Finally, I see the little bubbles that she is typing.

Thank you Ryder. For everything.

Goodnight, sweetheart, I respond and tuck my phone back into my cup holder. I pull at my pants to release the tightness against my ever-growing bulge. It's going to be a long night.

4

SIERRA

THE NEXT DAY, my phone dings toward the end of my shift. I have been working nonstop since I got here. But that's great for me tip-wise. Ryder was waiting outside of my apartment again this morning, ready to take me to work. It's been a busy shift, but my mind has been on Ryder all day.

While I'm walking to the back to fill up drinks, I pull out my phone and see I have a text from Ryder.

I'm running behind. I called you an Uber. She will be outside when you get off work. Sorry I couldn't pick you up.

And then another ding. He sent me a picture of the driver.

I text him back. *I can take the bus.*

I'd rather you didn't. It's already paid for. Be safe.

I think about it for a second, and decide I will talk to him about all this later. *Okay. Thank you!*

When I get off work, I find my driver waiting for me and willing to take me anywhere. I give her my address and go straight home. I can't help but think about the last few days, meeting Ryder, everything he's done to help me and then going out on a date with him. I'm ready for whatever our next step is. He's been a perfect gentleman and I appreciate him giving me time. It has been stressful, with work, school and everything with Johnny.

Once in my apartment, I've been in the door for a mere five minutes before the doorbell rings. Looking through the peephole, I see it's a UPS driver. When I open the door, he has me sign for a package and then carries in a huge box. I thank him and when he leaves, I look at the box. It's a sixty-five inch television. Oh my God! He's crazy. I can't accept this.

I immediately pick up the phone and dial his number. A woman picks up on the third ring.

"Uh, hi, uh, can I talk to Ryder?" I stutter into the phone.

The woman laughs, and I realize she is talking to someone else. When she comes back to the phone, she says, "He's busy right now, but let me get him for you."

"No, no," I stop her. "I will just talk to him later." And I hang up quickly.

My thoughts go wild, instantly wondering why a woman would be answering his phone. I take the rest of the afternoon to clean my apartment, then sit down with a peanut butter sandwich for dinner. I still haven't unboxed the television. I don't plan on keeping it.

Ryder has called me four times in the last hour. I didn't answer any of them. But I did listen to his messages and when I heard the worry in his voice, I did finally send him a text telling him I was fine.

Just as I pick up my sandwich, there is a knock on my door. I put my plate down and look out the peep hole. Ryder. I take a deep breath and unlock the door.

Opening it, I stand at the entrance. "Hey, Ryder."

"You didn't have the alarm set."

"But I'm awake and home. I don't need the alarm on."

He steps toward me and I instantly back up. "Can I come in?"

I shake my head. "Sure, yes, I'm sorry. Uh, I got your delivery today. Ryder, you can't buy me a television."

He just laughs. "I figured you wouldn't take it out of the box. Look, honey, it's not a big deal. I'm going to be over here more and I like to watch TV. No big deal."

"So you bought me a sixty-five-inch television? Why not a thirty-two? This is bigger than I would ever need."

"I like to watch sports on big TVs." He smiles broadly at me and shrugs. He starts unpacking it and stops when he sees my sandwich on the coffee table. He pulls out his phone and wallet. He calls a local pizza place and puts them on hold. "What do you like on your pizza?"

"Anything. But no anchovies or olives." And right then my belly growls.

"Got it." He finishes ordering and pays over the

phone. "It will be here shortly." He leans down and kisses me quickly, then goes back to the TV.

I should just keep my mouth shut, but I'm not that type of person. A woman answered his phone and if he has a girlfriend, I can't just keep kissing him.

"So I called you earlier," I mention as he is gets the remote out and starts going through the setup.

"Oh yeah? I tried calling you too." He smiles over at me.

I sit down on the couch and shrug my shoulders. "Yeah, uh, some woman answered your phone."

He sits down next to me, and I feel the heat of his body next to mine. I breathe in his manly scent but I can't look at him.

"That was Charlie. We work together. I leave my phone outside of the conference room so if there is an emergency, it can be answered. She knew to come and get me if you called. I will talk to her," he tells me with a stern voice.

"No, no, don't do that. It's not a big deal. I thought she was your girlfriend or something." I start to get up to go get a drink of water, or to just get up. I know I've embarrassed myself.

He grabs on to my hips and pulls me back down until I'm sitting on his lap. I try to get up. "Ryder, I'm too big to be sitting on your lap."

I stop struggling when he wraps his arm around me. "Don't say that. Look at us." And he points at the mirror on the wall.

I look into the mirror and he's right, sitting on his lap, I almost look small and dainty compared to him. I look at his broad shoulders, strong muscular arms covered in tattoos and also his big, muscular thighs that are holding me. When I raise my eyes back up to look at him in the mirror, I can see the heat in his eyes.

He tugs my chin to the side so he can whisper into my ear. "Charlie is definitely not my girlfriend. I don't have eyes for any woman besides you." And I feel his lips caress my ear lobe as he says it.

Ryder

I TURN her sideways to have better access to her mouth. This kiss is different than any kiss we've shared before. All the others were sweet, soft touches. This one I am devouring her mouth with my own. I want her to know that I want her and have no doubt about it whatsoever.

I open my eyes and look in the mirror at us. I pull away from her. "Look, honey, look at us now. Look how sexy you are."

Both of our eyes are hooded and lips swollen. Sierra's legs are spread wide, her skirt raised tight up her hips and I can see her panties, where proof of her desire has wet the cloth covering her most private parts. My hand strokes down her belly and rests between her thighs. I caress her slit through the wet cloth and she raises her hips to press into my hand. Pulling her panties to the side, I bare her pussy to me in the mirror. Damn, I could come just like this, just by looking at her swollen core as I penetrate through her slick folds. She leans back against me, giving me better access. I pull her shirt and bra up, exposing her almost fully to me. With one hand on her breast and one hand on her pussy, I watch her gyrate on my lap as she comes undone. She's begging me now, begging me to not stop and asking me for more.

I apply more pressure until her head is thrown back and her body tightens up as the climax takes ahold of her. Afterwards, she lies limply in my arms and I kiss her neck to soothe her. When I think she is almost asleep in my arms, she surprises me when she asks me "Will you take me, Ryder? I want you inside me."

"Yes, definitely." I set her on her feet, holding on to her until I know she is steady. When she's standing up, she finishes taking off her clothes until she is naked before me. I always thought I loved her curves, but there is nothing like seeing her naked curves.

I rush through undressing and then lift her into my arms and carry her to her bedroom. I lay her down on the bed and cuddle next to her, kissing her with my cock hard and pressed against her thigh.

"I'm clean, honey. I want to be in you bare," I tell her between kisses.

"I'm clean too. I've only had sex once..."

"No, honey, I don't want to hear about others," I insist.

As I'm kissing her, she's pressing her body off the bed, trying to lead me to her pussy.

I line myself up at her center and slowly enter her. She's tight, oh so tight and my cock feels like it's in a vice grip. I grip the sheets on each side of her, trying to stay in control and not let myself slam into her with one thrust. I work my way into her tight channel slowly and with each inch I go, she's moaning my name, begging me for more. It feels like the blood is rushing through my head, I've never felt this much desire or ecstasy before. Damn, what is she doing to me?

I blink a few times to clear my vision and, unable to hold back any longer, I slam into her roughly until I'm buried deeply inside her and my balls are hitting her butt. With each plunge inside her, we both moan.

"Sierra, honey, you feel so good," I moan into her mouth between kisses. I lift her legs up and press them against her sides. I'm able to go deeper and I thrust inside her until she's screaming my name and we both climax at the same time. I shoot my load deep inside her womb and I don't come out until I'm completely done, and even then, I'm wanting to stay inside her.

Once we catch our breath, I roll off of her and pull her into my arms. I end up deep inside her three more times throughout the night. And I still can't get enough.

5

SIERRA

It's been two weeks since Johnny stole my stuff and I met Ryder. Ryder has gone out of his way to protect me. He admitted to me that first night we had sex that he had been staying in his truck outside my apartment to make sure I was okay. We have spent every night since then either at my apartment or his house. If we are not at work or I'm not in school, then we are together.

He was disappointed when he found out I was on the pill. He thought for sure that he was breeding me. I gasped in astonishment when he told me that. It's tempting though. I do love the idea of having his babies.

Tonight I'm going over to his house. I had to stop by

mine to grab some clothes. I no longer take the bus; he has loaned me one of his cars to drive. I tried to refuse him, but he won me over.

Walking through the apartment, I grab a few changes of clothes and my makeup and stuff. When I hear the doorbell, I smile, thinking that it's probably Ryder. I run through the apartment and swing open the door. And to my surprise, Johnny is standing there. His pungent smell hits me as soon as I open the door. He looks rough and I want to cry when I think about what he must be going through.

"Johnny, what are you doing here?"

"Hey, sis, can I come in?" He started calling me that back in high school. It used to make me feel special, like I had two big brothers. But not anymore.

I hesitate briefly, knowing that Ryder would not want me to let him in. But if I plan on getting him help, I have to.

"Sure, come on in. I was just getting ready to leave, but I can talk for a few minutes."

He walks in and sits on my couch. I sit on the chair across from him and ask him how he's doing.

"I'm fine."

I know he's lying. He looks worse than I've ever seen him. "I'm going to get a drink," I say. "Do you want something?"

"Sure, whatever." He shrugs.

I walk into the kitchen and grab my phone off the counter to send Ryder a text. *Johnny is here. In my apartment. I'm okay.*

I grab some bottles of water out of the refrigerator and look at my phone when it dings. *I'm on my way.*

Putting my phone back into my pocket, I walk back into the living room. Johnny is standing in front of my TV looking at it appreciatively. I instantly get mad with the reminder that he took my old one.

"Why are you here, Johnny?"

He looks all around me and won't look into my face. "I need some money, Sierra."

"I don't think…" I start to tell him I don't think it's a good idea I give him money but he interrupts me.

"I wouldn't ask you if I didn't really need it. I'm in trouble, sis. I need your help."

"You need to go to rehab, Johnny. You need to get off the drugs. It's killing you. I mean, just look at you." I can't help myself; I have to tell him the truth.

I see the rage in his eyes and I realize then that I don't even know him anymore. He's not the same person and I could kick myself for letting him in.

"You don't understand. I don't have a problem. Now are you going to help me or not?" He's leaned over top of me on the couch and he's looking at me menacingly. I never dreamed in a million years that I would ever be afraid of him.

"She's not," I hear right before Johnny is pulled away from me. Ryder must have come in while Johnny was standing over me. His face is livid and his whole body is taut, veins bulging out of his neck and arms.

"Who the hell do you think you are?" he screams as he slams his fist into Johnny's face.

Johnny just takes it and I have to get in front of Ryder to stop him before he kills him.

"Ryder, Ryder." I keep saying his name with my hands on each side of his face. It's like he is in a trance and I'm trying to wake him up. I lean up and kiss his lips. "I'm okay, Ryder. I'm okay. Please stop."

Ryder grabs on to my hips and pulls me toward him, holding me until his breathing evens out. "I'm calling the police." He pulls his phone out of his pocket but I grab it from him.

"Ryder, listen. This isn't the same boy that was my brother's best friend. But I know he's in there. I know if he got help, if he would just accept help, he could be okay."

He thinks about it for only a second. "I won't put you in jeopardy, honey. If he doesn't agree to be committed to rehab then I am calling the police. I won't bend on this."

"Okay," I tell him before I kiss him one more time.

It took some convincing, but finally after Ryder threatened him and laid on the guilt for everything he had done to me, his dead best friend's little sister, he agreed. Some of the things that Ryder said were pretty harsh, but obviously something that Johnny needed to hear.

Ryder had me drive over to his house to wait while he took Johnny to the hospital. Ryder had it all arranged by the time they got there. He stayed and helped him get admitted with the promise to bring him some clothes the next day. When Ryder finally got home, I was waiting for him naked in his bed.

Instead of trying to have sex with me, he just held me in his arms. "I don't know what I would do if something had happened to you tonight," he whispers in my ear.

I thought about that too, while I was waiting on him to get home. There's so much I haven't said to him that I know I should. "I love you, Ryder. I've loved you for a while now and I just want you to know."

"I love you…"

I interrupt him before he finishes. "You don't have to say it just because I did. I was thinking the same thing tonight and I was wishing that you knew I loved you."

He smiles and rolls away from me, getting something from the table by the bed. When he rolls back, he has a small box in his hands that he holds out to me. "I love you, too, Sierra. I've wanted to tell you for a while now, but I didn't want to scare you off. I know you thought this was moving fast. But I want you to know that I plan to spend the rest of my life with you. You've changed me. You make me happy… You make me want to be a better man. You make me want to be a daddy. Please, honey, will you marry me?"

By this time the tears are rolling down my face and I can't stop them. "Yes, yes, I would love to be your wife and give you babies."

EPILOGUE

SIERRA

HE DIDN'T GIVE me any time to reconsider. His words not mine. He moved all my stuff in the very next day while I was in class. We finally set a date. I had planned on having a longer engagement to let me finish school but he had other plans. He said I could just finish school as his wife. I only have a year and a half until I'm done. He is counting down, because we both agreed I should finish school before the babies came.

We are being married exactly three months after we met. That was the longest he would give me to plan everything. Charlie, the woman that works with him, is my maid of honor. We've become close since I've met her and it's funny the way she calls Ryder out. She's braver than most men, I have come to realize.

At the wedding, I have Ryder's best friend and partner, Mike, walk me down the aisle. When we stop right in front of Ryder, he doesn't wait for the preacher to ask 'Who gives this woman?' He reaches over and grabs me out of Mike's arm.

I gently slap him on the chest like he's in trouble, but honestly that's one of my favorite things about him, the way he's so possessive of me.

We say our vows before our friends and it's over before we know it. Ryder swings me up into his arms and carries me out of the church, promising me forever.

EPILOGUE 2

RYDER

Three Years Later

THE LAST THREE years have been the best of my life. Sierra has made all my dreams come true. We agreed to wait to have children until she had finished school but she decided to surprise me and go off the pill her last year, thinking it would take her a while to get pregnant. Well, she ended up getting pregnant right away.

She was sick the first few months and I felt horrible for her. But she is such a trooper. She always bounced right back. I went to every appointment and I admit I cried when I saw our baby on the ultrasound screen for the first time.

"You okay, Daddy?" she asked me with a big grin. I

still think back to that moment, when it finally set in that I was going to be a dad.

She took her last exam one week before our little Ellie was born. And today, we are celebrating her second birthday. She has been the light of both of our lives and I have to admit she has me wrapped around her finger.

But not just me, Uncle Johnny too. Johnny did finish rehab. He put in the work and got clean. He still apologizes to Sierra sometimes about what he did to her, but she just shrugs it away. She's not one to hold grudges. Our little Ellie loves him and calls him Uncle Johnny. And he has changed just being around her.

Don't get me wrong. It was hard in the beginning when he first got out. I didn't trust him with Sierra and then Ellie. I mean, they are my world, my everything. But he understood. He was only allowed to visit when I was around. Since he's been out, I have given him a job at Alpha Security and he has proven to me over and over that I can trust him to be right with my family.

"Daddy, are you going to help me blow out my candles?" Ellie asks me in a sing-song voice.

"You know I am, baby. I can't wait." I scoop her up and carry her toward my wife, my love, Sierra holding out the birthday cake with two candles on it. She sets it on the table and no sooner sets it down than Ellie jumps up into her arms. Sierra slides her around to her hip. "Make a wish, baby girl."

Ellie squeals and leans down to blow out her candles. I meet my wife's eyes over our daughter's head and I can already see the desire in her eyes. "Tonight," I mouth to her.

And she shakes her head at me and leans in for a kiss.

THE END

PROTECTING WHAT'S MINE

1

CHARLIE

IT NEVER FAILS. I'm just trying to do my job and some man thinks because I have my butt in the air, he can touch it. This is the second time this week and I've had enough. You would think people these days would know the rules, as in, don't touch a woman without asking first. Definitely don't fondle her ass while she's at your work trying to install a new alarm system.

I knew the moment I met him that he would be a problem. He started hitting on me the moment I walked in the door. I refused his advances and I even did it politely. But my politeness is about to wear off.

I'm at Knox Tavern on the west side of town. This is their second restaurant in the area and my boss, Ryder, sent me here to do the new install. *It will be easy*, he said. Biting the inside of my cheek, I try to push down my irritation.

His name is Kevin. And I am guessing he thinks he is God's gift to women. He's the type that thinks just because I'm a curvy, plus-size woman, I should be falling at his feet. Well, I'm not and I won't be. However, he is not accepting my brush-off and he is becoming more persistent.

He asked me to meet him in an office in the back of the restaurant. I said no and insisted on a table out in the open. He asked me out and I told him no. The back of his hand touched my breast when he handed back the paperwork I had given him to sign and I called him out on it. He said it was an accident. However, I'm under a desk resetting a modem and his hand caresses my ass and stays there until I stand up. He has his body pressed tightly against my back and I try not to lose my temper as I turn around and push him backwards.

Grabbing up my things, I start shoving them into my bag. I refuse to finish the install with this vile man in my presence. I will come back later when the owner or another manager is here. Throwing my bag over my shoulder, I head to the door. Until Jackass Kevin decides to give it another try.

"Stop, honey, don't go. Finish the installation. Then you and I can go get a drink."

"No thank you. I will just come back another day. Maybe when your boss is here." I clench my teeth to stop myself from telling him exactly what I want to say to him.

He grips my shoulder tightly. "Look, my boss expected this to be done today. You are not leaving until it's done."

I can feel my pulse elevating. "You should have thought about that before you decided to feel me up, asshole." And I pull away from him.

He brushes past me and presses me against the open door of the office. "Now look, honey..."

But I don't give him time to finish. I lift my knee to his groin and as he doubles over in pain, I take the opportunity to get out of here.

I can still hear him moaning as I run out the front door.

Serves him right.

I stop on my way back to the office and grab a coffee. Decaf, of course. I don't need any caffeine at this point.

When I walk into the office, I immediately hear Mike, one of the owners, hollering my name and calling me into his office.

When I walk in, I calmly sit down and I can tell by the look on his face, Knox Tavern has already called him.

"Charlie, the new install at Knox Tavern was supposed to be completed today. Brody, the owner, called and is upset that you walked out in the middle of a job."

I keep quiet and just stare Mike down. He is a great boss and usually very reasonable. But of course, I've never ticked off one of his clients before, either.

"So... are you going to tell me what happened? It's not like you to not finish a job."

Biting my lip, I decide I may as well confess. It will come out eventually. "I kneed Kevin, one of the managers, in the groin, sir."

"You did what?" he explodes and jumps up from his seat. He's holding his hands to his temple and I can see his thoughts racing. When he gets himself together, he finally asks me, "So why exactly did you knee him in the groin?" And he grimaces when he says the word groin.

"Well, he wouldn't take no for an answer. I didn't want to get a drink with him, I didn't want his hand on my breast or my ass. I had enough and took care of it... sir."

"Quit with the sir, Charlie. You never call me that. Are you okay?" At the shake of my head, he continues, "I knew there was an explanation. I will take care of it."

"No. I have already taken care of it. I will finish the job. I will just go back when Kevin isn't working, no big deal."

He looks at me worriedly. "But are you okay? I can..."

"Mike. I'm fine. There is nothing to take care of. I can take care of myself. I will go back and finish the job."

"No. I will put Johnny on it. He will take care of it." He runs his hand through his hair.

"You can't send someone else. Surely I have proven to you that I can handle it. I will take care of it. It will be done before close of business tomorrow. Now, is there anything else you need? I have work to do." I appreciate him wanting to help me, but I can take care of myself. I've been doing it a long time.

He hesitates, wanting to say more. "No. That's all."

I walk out of his office and toward mine. Wow, it's been a long day.

Brody

OPENING A NEW BUSINESS IS STRESSFUL. There are a hundred things on my list and I take joy in checking things off.

Today, the new security system was supposed to be installed. And it wasn't.

Kevin said that Charlie, a new representative, was here but left before the job was done. I instantly called Mike, one of the owners of Alpha Security. He assured me that Charlie is not usually like that and something must have come up, but he guaranteed that the install would be complete by tomorrow.

I move security system to tomorrow's list and start looking at what still needs to be finished today.

Frustrated when the phone rings, interrupting me, I answer it gruffly. "Hello."

"Brody. This is Mike, with Alpha Security. I wanted to let you know I talked to Charlie. She explained why she left before the job was complete and I wanted to talk to you about it."

"Sure. So Charlie is a woman?"

"Yes. She is one of our best installers, actually. That's why I was so surprised that she had left before the job was done," he tells me.

"Okay, so I'm pretty busy, and I don't have time to gossip, Mike. What happened?" I try to rush him along.

His tone changes instantly. "Sure, I'll get right to it. Your manager Kevin harassed her and she left. However, I assure you that the job will be done by tomorrow at close of business. Charlie insists that she will complete the job, but if Kevin is going to be there, I will have to insist that someone else take over your install."

It's like my mind closes down after he said 'harrassed.' I sputter, "What do you mean 'harrassed'?"

Impatient now, Mike grunts into the phone, "Well, he touched her breast and then grabbed her ass when she was bent over in the office trying to install a new modem. She kept trying to politely turn him down, but he wasn't taking no for an answer. So she kneed him in the nuts. Which I might add, he deserved. So all I need to know is, will he be there tomorrow?"

I put up with a lot from people, but I never allow someone to get away with mistreating a woman. My hands clench and unclench, my heart pounding erratically. "I assure you, Kevin will not be here tomorrow or any day after. I do not permit such things in my restaurant and I definitely don't ever permit anyone to treat a woman in such a way. Please, have her come tomorrow. I will be here."

Mike is quiet on the other end for a moment, until I hear him take a deep breath. "I thought you would say that. Thanks, Brody. Honestly, she can take care of herself, but I didn't want to put her into that situation. She will be there tomorrow."

Once I hang up, incensed, I rise from my seat and walk to the kitchen in search of Kevin. He's sitting in the break room with an ice pack pressed against his privates. My blood boiling, I tell him, "You have three minutes to get your things and get out. You are fired."

"Fired? What for?" he sputters at me.

"Why are you holding an ice pack to your dick, Kevin?"

His face turns red and he can't wipe the guilty expression off his face fast enough. "Look, she was into it."

Grabbing him by the collar, I've heard enough and I tell him so. "That's it. No more. I won't tolerate you treating a woman this way. Get out. You will be lucky if I don't convince her to press charges."

"The fat bitch wanted it," he snarls in my face and I stare him down, barely holding on to my anger.

"Out. Now." I drag him to the back door and throw him out into the alley.

It takes a long time to calm down, but when I finally do, I know that I owe a big apology to Charlie. I forget about my list of things that need to be done and I go home.

2

CHARLIE

Last night was like any other night. I went home alone, ate dinner and went to bed. I'm twenty-five years old and live my life on my own terms. I have no desire to date. Most of the men I have known, with the exception of the men at Alpha Security, have shown me how unreliable they can be. Starting with my father who left when I was only two years old. Then, when my mother passed away when I was five, I was shipped around to ten different foster homes. I was never adopted and eventually aged out of the system. Being alone is all I've ever known.

Getting dressed this morning, I put on my black Alpha Security uniform. I grab a cup of coffee and head out the door. Thinking about yesterday, I hope that I am not going to have to deal with Kevin again today. I had heard such good things about the people of Knox Tavern, I was a little surprised that someone like Kevin was working for them. I've never backed down before and I'm a little disappointed in myself that I didn't finish the job yesterday. I should have kneed him in the nuts and then completed the project while he moaned in pain. Pulling my shoulders back, I put my game face on.

I'm here today and no matter what, I won't leave until it's finished.

"Hello," I call out when I walk in the front door.

"I'll be right there," a voice hollers out from the back.

Standing there with my bag over my shoulder, I decide to go to the back to the sound of the voice. "I'm Charlie, from Alpha Security. I'm here to finish your..." But I don't finish. A man comes around the corner and I stop, stunned at the sight before me.

A man, a large man with dark brown hair and beautiful eyes, is looking back at me. Even from here I can tell his eyes are a bright blue, probably the bluest eyes I've ever seen.

He towers over my five-foot-six frame and I tilt my head backwards to look up at him because he doesn't stop coming toward me until he's standing right in front of me.

"Charlie. You're Charlie?" he huskily asks me and I can't help but notice the vein in the side of his neck vibrating against his skin.

"Yes." I clear my throat. "Yes, I'm here to finish the install. I apologize for leaving yesterday, Mr...."

"Call me Brody. And you don't have anything to apologize for. It's me that should be apologizing. I don't tolerate anyone mistreating women and I'm sorry that happened to you."

"It's not a big deal. I'm going to get started," I say, trying to change the subject.

"It is a big deal. No woman, especially you, deserves to be treated like that. I've fired Kevin. He won't bother you again," he assures me.

"Uh, okay, thank you," I tell him, confused. I've never been treated like this before, and I have to stop myself from tearing up because I realize this man that I just met has looked out for me more than any other man of my life. *Geez, Charlie, get it together.*

He keeps looking at me, and I can see the look in his eyes. Like he feels sorry for me.

I take my eyes off him and walk away. From him and

the conversation. It's too serious for me, especially this early in the morning.

Walking into the back, I get to work. But no matter how hard I try, I can't get my mind off the blue-eyed hottie in the front.

Brody

FUCK. That's all I can think when I watch Charlie's wide hips sway as she walks into my office. The poor woman had to put up with Kevin hitting on her yesterday and now I have to reel myself in before I make the same mistake. But it's hard, in every sense of the word. Charlie is pure perfection. She's curvy, just the way I like them. Her long blond hair is up in a ponytail and it sways back and forth as she walks. I can't get the memory of her deep green eyes out of my head. Every emotion she felt was shining through them. Anger when she was talking about Kevin, sadness when I said I had fired him and I'm not positive, but I'm pretty sure I saw desire in her eyes before she quickly walked away from me.

I have so much to do today, but I know at this point, I'm not going to get any of it done while I'm in such close proximity to my dream girl. She is every fantasy I've ever had and I don't plan to let her escape so easily.

I work most of the morning in my office, just so I can be around her. I catch her looking at me when she thinks I don't see her. By midmorning, my cock is hard in my pants as I watch her ass in the air. I have to will it down, just because of everything she went through yesterday. I don't want her to compare me to Kevin.

"So I think that's it. Everything is set up. You have the same system at your restaurant downtown, so I assume you don't need me to show you the cameras and how to view them?" she asks me.

"Uh, do you mind showing me? Just to make sure I have it."

"Absolutely. Can I use your computer?" she asks me as she gestures to my desk.

I nod at her and stand to the side so she can sit down. "You just log in here. I have your username and password on the paperwork. Once you're logged in, you click here to see the different camera angles."

I bend down and lean over her shoulder to watch her move around on the screen. I know this software. We have used it for the last year at our other location, but I needed a reason to keep her here longer. I breathe in the scent of her and I swear she smells like coconut and sugar.

"Have you got it? Any questions?" I would think she felt like I was just another client, until I see the telltale sign of her desire when she is holding her breath and her tongue darts out and slides across her lips.

"Yes, I got it." I have her caged in, one hand on the desk and one hand on the back of her chair. I'm holding her gaze with mine and all of a sudden she looks away.

"Okay, I'm going to go then. If you will sign this I will be out of your way." She hands me a paper and pen.

Holding the paper in my hands, I look over at her and a blush covers her cheeks.

"Are you in a hurry to go home?" I ask her while I bend down to sign the paper.

"No, no hurry, but I'm going back to the office." Our hands touch when I hand her back the pen. Her eyes snap up to mine and I know she felt it too. The attraction is there, no doubt about it.

"Will you go out to dinner with me?" I ask her. I tell myself if she says no, that I won't pressure her. But a part of me knows that I can't just let her walk out of here.

I see the surprise in her eyes and she starts to say, "Uh, I don't think that's a good..."

But I interrupt her. "Please, just dinner. I owe you for everything that you went through yesterday."

She looks disappointed for a minute, but then pulls herself together. "I'm used to men like Kevin. I haven't thought about him since. There is no reason to apologize for his behavior. Now, if that's why you want to take me out, I have to say no. Thank you, but no."

She's feisty. And I like it. I put my hand on hers and pull it between the two of mine. "That's not the only reason I asked you out. I want to go out with you. I want to take you to dinner." I want to bend her over my desk and make her mine, but decide to leave that part out. I feel like I need to move slowly with her and I'm determined not to mess this up.

3

CHARLIE

I CAN'T BELIEVE I agreed to go out with him. I never date a client. I'm sure there is some kind of rule against it, but when I asked Mike about it, he said that Brody had already called him and threatened him to not discourage me from going on a date with him. So Mike assured me it was okay, no rules are being broken. It makes me smile thinking that Brody was worried I would try to back out of the date.

I go through my closet and decide on my green A-line dress, the one that matches my eyes. It's not like I haven't dated before. I have. But this seems different and it sort of freaks me out. I don't want a commitment. Yes, I've had sex before, but honestly just to scratch an itch. I've never been in a relationship before, and I don't want to be.

The doorbell rings and I take one last glance at myself in the mirror, blow the hair out of my face and go to answer it.

Brody is leaning against my door jamb and I take in his holy hotness with my mouth hanging open. He's wearing dark jeans, a white T-shirt that is stretched across his muscled chest and a leather jacket. Almost instantly, my body tingles and my panties are wet. Damn, I hope I can make it through dinner without jumping on him.

"You look beautiful, Charlie," he tells me as he glances down my body, stopping briefly at my cleavage on display.

"Thank you. You look... handsome." Heat floods my face because I almost told him he looked hot.

He grabs on to my hand and laces his fingers with mine. "You ready to go?"

I nod at him and pull my purse up on my shoulder. I lock the door and walk out to his SUV.

Dinner is excellent and he is a gentleman throughout the whole evening. He helps me into the car, holds doors open, pulls chairs out for me, and buys my dinner. The conversation never stops. He tells me about how he started his restaurants and his plans to add on more. He asks about me and what made me join Alpha Security. I explain to him that that I applied to be a security guard but Mike has me starting on the security system side until I get more training.

"What about your family? Do they live close by?" he asks me.

"No. Uh, I was raised in foster care. No family," I tell him and then tell him no big deal when he apologizes to me.

Quickly changing the subject, I ask him more about him.

Before I know it, we've finished our dinner of steaks and baked potatoes. Throughout the whole meal, Brody had his hands on me in some way or another. Even when he was eating, he still had his hand wrapped around mine. Needless to say, my panties are soaked and I'm almost panting in heat wanting him.

He's so handsome. I don't get the vibe that he is a player, but maybe he is. What am I saying, what do I care? I don't do relationships and am not interested in starting one now. Maybe I can have him one night and I'm hoping tonight is the night.

He walks me to my door and I unlock it. I'm about to ask him in when he says, "I had a great time tonight, Charlie. Will you go out with me again?"

I try to hide my disappointment. I don't want the night to end, but I'm also not going to throw myself at him. "Yes, sure."

He leans down and kisses my forehead lightly before walking away.

Brody

DETERMINED NOT to fuck this up, I force myself to walk away. What I want is to take her inside and make her mine. And I saw it in her eyes, she would have let me. She wanted it. There's no doubt about it. And if she was anyone else, I would have done it. But I don't want to fuck this up and move too fast. I want to do this right.

The next week, I either talk to or see Charlie every day. We go to the movies, out to dinner, she helps me paint at the restaurant when a painter doesn't show up and we go work out together. By the end of the week, I have blue balls and I know I can't take another day of seeing her in her black tight leggings at the gym. She doesn't even realize it, but there are a number of men watching her on the treadmill as she walks. Running next to her, I grip the bars tight and give a threatening look to every man that looks her way.

The gym is on the same street as my restaurant downtown. We stop in to eat and for me to check in on things.

Holding her hand, I ask her what she's doing later. "I was thinking I would cook you dinner and you could come to my apartment." She smiles shyly at me, and I see the lust in her face.

"Honey, dinner sounds great, but I don't trust myself alone with you," I tell her as I raise her hand to my lips.

"Why not? I'm ready, Brody. I want you," she says with her eyes sparkling.

I moan, and instantly cover my dick with my hand to rearrange my growing bulge. "I want you too, honey. But once I have you, you're mine. Are you ready for that?"

She pulls back from me, almost like I've slapped her. Her eyes are huge and I see the fear in them. "No, that wasn't the deal." She leans across the table and starts whispering loudly to me, "I want you, but I can't have a relationship with you."

"Why not? What's wrong with me?" I ask her now, offended.

"What? Nothing's wrong with you. I just don't do relationships." She starts to get up from the table, but I stop her by putting my hand on hers.

"I have to go, Brody," she says.

"Well, well, no wonder you fired me." We both look up and see Kevin standing by the table. He's looking between us and he stares at Charlie longer than I'm comfortable with. I slide out of the booth and block him from looking at her.

"What do you want, Kevin?" I ask him, frustrated.

"I'm here to pick up my last check," he says, still trying to look at Charlie.

At this point, patrons at the other tables are looking at us and I'm trying not to cause a scene. "Okay, come into the back and I will get it for you."

"No, that's okay, I have unfinished business with Charlie. I'll wait here." He steps around me.

I grab him by the collar, and lean in to whisper to him, "You're lucky to share the same air she breathes, asshole, but I'm not leaving you out here with her."

"That won't be a problem. I'm leaving," Charlie announces and slides from the booth.

Kevin reaches out for her and instinctively, I grab his hand and squeeze it in mine before he ever reaches her.

"I can take care of myself, Brody. I can definitely handle him." She gestures to Kevin, who is hunched over in pain because I still haven't let go of his hand.

"That's just It, honey. You can take care of yourself. I know it. You know it. But as long as I'm around, you don't have to. I protect what's mine. And I know you don't realize it yet, but, honey you are mine," I tell her and hold her gaze so she knows how sincere I am.

She squeezes her eyes shut, and when she opens them I can see the fear and panic in them. She runs from the restaurant. I want to follow her and demand that she stay. But she's not like that. If I demand anything of her, she will do the exact opposite. I decide the best thing to do is let her calm down. So, instead of chasing her, I take care of paying Kevin and then taking the trash out. Literally.

4

_____

CHARLIE

I ALMOST HYPERVENTILATE by the time I make it back to my car. Once there, I sit and try to get ahold of my emotions. Brody has scared me to death. I can feel the hope rising inside me just wondering how good it could be with him, but then the fear of losing him overwhelms me and I almost lose my lunch.

I drive straight home and cry myself to sleep on the couch. Crying is something I haven't let myself do since I was five years old and my mother died. But I give in and let it all out until I'm exhausted.

I wake up when the sun has set, and someone is pounding on my door. Looking through the peephole, I see it's him. Brody.

Opening the door, I realize that I probably look a

mess. "Oh, honey," he says and wraps his arms around me. I snuggle into his chest and breathe in his manly scent. He picks me up and carries me to the couch, sitting down with me in his lap.

"Honey, you are breaking my heart. No more crying," he pleads with me.

In response, all I do is sniff and bury myself deeper into his chest. He strokes my hair and I just revel in being in his arms. I haven't ever allowed myself to do this. Be comforted by someone. I can't remember ever being held like this.

"Tell me what happened back there. Why did you panic when I said you are mine?" he asks me.

I take a deep breath and try to collect my thoughts. "I told you I was raised in foster care, didn't I?"

"Yes," he huskily replies.

"Well, my dad left me when I was only two. My mom died when I was five. I went from foster home to foster home until I finally aged out of the system. I never... never had anyone in my corner. And I've learned to depend on myself, to take care of myself. Now, I'm just programmed that way, Brody. I can't lean on you, I can't depend on you to be there for me. I won't let myself. All I have to give you is one night."

"Honey, I want more," he tells me and I feel my heart breaking in my chest. Oh how I wish I could give that to him.

We sit in silence, him stroking my hair and my back. I have cold chills up my arms and I wrap them around him. I touch my lips to his neck and I feel him stiffen underneath me. But I don't stop. I kiss up his neck, then his earlobe and he sucks in his breath. But I still don't stop, moving across his jawline with sweet little kisses until I stop on his lips. When my lips touch his, he's frozen under me and I know I can't let myself stop now. I pull back and look into his eyes. His usual light blue eyes are dark with desire. I shift on his lap and I feel the hardness of his cock pressed against my bottom. He moans when I shift against him and I lean in, meeting him halfway to kiss him again.

He takes control and deepens the kiss. Our lips are tangled together and the palm of his hand is pressed against my back, pulling me toward him. I briefly stand up and then sit down again, straddling him, never letting our lips break apart. His hands go to my thighs and his hard length is pressed against my core. My hips gyrate against him, wanting him, begging for a release.

He pulls away and rests his head against mine. His breathing is erratic and I can tell he is trying to get control of himself. But that's not what I want. I want him to lose all control with me.

"Don't stop, Brody. Don't stop. I want this. I want you," I plead as I grind against him.

Groaning, he answers, "I want you, too. But once I'm in your tight pussy, that will seal your fate, honey. You will be mine. Until you realize that, until you are willing to be mine, I can't do it."

I'm barely hanging on here. I'm so out of my mind wanting to come that I almost promise him everything he wants. But reality hits me and I know I can't do it. I don't do relationships. He must be reading my mind, because then he tells me, "Don't worry, honey. We will get there."

Even though I know we won't, I still see the hope in his eyes and I want to believe him. I very badly want to believe him.

"You need to come, don't you, baby?" he asks me as he lifts his hips up and presses his hard cock against me.

"Yes, please, yes," I beg him.

He lifts me up like I weigh nothing and lays me down on the couch. In one fluid motion, he has my sleep shorts and underwear down my legs and on the floor. I'm bare to him from the waist down.

I'm wet, soaked. He spreads my legs wider, one on the floor and one on the back of the couch.

When he touches the inside of my thigh, I about come undone. He strokes through my slick folds and when I moan his name, he bends down and kisses my mound. His tongue slides across my opening and then he focuses on my wet, swollen bundle of nerves.

"Come for me, baby." He moans against me and instantly my hips are shaking uncontrollably, my hand holding his head to me as I ride out my release.

Brody

MY PLAN IS to give her the release she needs, then get the hell out of here. A man is only so strong and looking at her right now, it wouldn't take much for me to give in. She's satiated, her eyes are hooded and her pleasure is evident on her face. I lean over and kiss her before cuddling her in my arms and picking her up. I carry her, lying limply in my arms, to her room awkwardly because it's like I have a steel rod in my pants pressing against my zipper. I lay her gently on the bed, pull the covers up over her and sit beside her. She opens her eyes and looks up at me.

"Brody, I can't do forever. No matter how much I want to," she whispers sadly to me.

I don't want to ruin the night and I know she's not really in the mood to talk right now. "I won't take anything less with you."

She starts to argue, but I put my finger across her lips. "We will talk tomorrow. Sweet dreams, baby girl. I'll lock the door on my way out." I kiss her one last time and leave.

Walking to my truck, I tug at my jeans. I sit and try to calm myself down. If I was any less of a man, I would have taken what Charlie was willing to give. But that's not enough for me. I want it all. And I want it with her.

5
———

CHARLIE

THE NEXT MORNING, I wake up well rested, but my eyes are still swollen from crying. I drive to the office and when I walk in, the receptionist, Carrie, jumps up from her desk and comes around to me. "What's wrong? What happened?"

I shake my head at her and go to my office. No sooner do I sit down than Carrie comes in and shuts the door.

"Charlie, I know you like to keep things to yourself and whatever, but your face is as white as a ghost. Talk to me, let me help you."

After years of being on my own, I have two people wanting to help me in the span of two days. A tear slips down my face and I wipe at it quickly. What is wrong with me? For someone that never cries, I've turned into a blubbering mess.

"I, uh, don't even know where to begin," I tell her honestly.

"How about the beginning?" she suggests.

"I, uh, started seeing a guy and ..."

"Brody, from Knox Tavern?" she interrupts.

Biting my lip, I ask her, "How did you know that?"

"One day he called here and raised hell about him taking you out and that Mike had to tell you it was okay. So I just assumed..."

"Yep, that's him. He' pretty bossy and possessive," I assure her.

"He sounds hot." She giggles and then covers her mouth to stifle it.

I nod at her. He definitely is that. "Well, he wants me... to be his."

Her eyebrows come together in confusion. "His? Like his booty call, his girlfriend, wife, what does that mean?"

"His... I don't know... his – forever," I stutter out and then lay my head down on the desk.

"I don't get it. What's the problem? A lot of men are looking for one night – and he is telling you he wants forever?"

At my nod to let her know she understands correctly, she asks, "And you don't like him?"

"No, I do like him. I like him a lot." I smile thinking about him last night, how patient and unselfish he was.

"So what's the problem?" At this point, Carrie is exasperated.

"Knock, knock," Mike calls out and opens my office door. "Everything okay in here?" He looks between Carrie and me.

"Yes, yes, everything is fine," I assure him. "What can I do for you?"

He's looking at Carrie and her face blushes a bright red. When he looks over at me, he says, "Just a reminder we are meeting with the new clients in ten. See you in the conference room. Bye, Carrie," he says before walking out and shutting the door behind him.

Carrie keeps looking at the door and her face is even more flushed than it was before.

"You like him!" I accuse her.

Alarmed, she looks back at me. "What? No – uh – what does it matter? I've liked him forever and he's never noticed me. I'm not exactly his type." She gestures down her body.

I take a good look at Carrie and I want to ask her why she dresses the way she does. I think she's great, she's funny and beautiful. She could get Mike if she tried. But she wears clothes that are three sizes too big for her, she never wears makeup and her long red hair is always up in a bun. If she put in a little effort, I'm sure Mike would notice her. Any man would.

"Anyway, we are not talking about me. What's the problem? You like Brody. He likes you," she asks, changing the subject.

"I don't do relationships. I can't – with my past – I just don't want to depend on someone else," I mutter.

"I get it. I do. Relationships are scary. And unpredictable. We've all been hurt and you don't want to put yourself out there. But, Charlie, if he loves you and you love him, you have to trust him."

I keep shaking my head the longer she talks. Just the thought of it, giving my heart to someone, freaks me out.

"Okay, okay," she says, holding her hands out in front of her. "Can you picture the rest of your like without him in it?"

I shrug my shoulders.

"Can you imagine never speaking to him again? Not seeing him?" she asks me.

I hesitate. I can't even lift my shoulders to shrug this time because I'm picturing a world where he's not it. I fall back in my chair, thinking about what she said.

She gets up and with one hand on the door, she stops and turns around. "Men like him don't come around every day. If you feel about him like I think you do, then don't give up on him. More importantly, don't give up on yourself."

When she walks out the door, I sit here thinking, wondering if it can be as easy as she suggests. Can I make a decision to just let it happen? Lost in thought, I startle when my phone dings, reminding me of my meeting.

Brody

TONIGHT IS the opening of my new restaurant and all I can think about is Charlie. She's avoiding me. No doubt about it. I've sent her flowers and candy. I've tried texting her and calling her with no response. I've tried tracking her down, but it's almost like she's disappeared. I texted Johnny, one of the men over at Alpha Security, three days ago and he said she's fine. I even called Carrie, the secretary, today to try and check in on her and she said to just give her time, she'll come around.

I do know that she's reading my texts. They all say they've been read. So I don't give up. It's been a week. But it feels like it's been forever. I scroll through my texts from the last seven days.

I can't get anything done. All I do is think of you, I sent the first day.

I miss holding your hand. Yours fit perfectly in mine, I sent the second day.

I would give anything to see your smile today, I sent the third day.

A woman hit on me today. I told her I was taken. God, I miss you, I sent the fourth day.

I wish I could kiss you goodnight and hold you in my arms. Sweet dreams, I sent the fifth day.

I love you. Did I tell you that? Nothing is going to change my mind on that, I sent the sixth day.

And today, well, today I open the restaurant and I'm excited and nervous. But more than anything, I wish I could share it with her. So I text her again.

The restaurant is opening in an hour. But I don't care. It means nothing if I can't share it with you. I miss you.

I do all the last-minute things that need done. I smile like I'm supposed to and shake hands with people and network like I'm supposed to. But all I want to do is go find Charlie.

I'm talking to a few of the employees in the corner when something catches my eye. I gasp. Charlie is standing at the entrance and almost instantly her gaze is on me. Her hair is in curls, lying down her back. She is dressed in a tight black dress that shows off her curves.

I walk away from my employees and stalk over to her, not stopping until I'm standing right in front of her. "You came," I say to her softly.

She bites her lip, her eyes never leaving mine. "I wanted to see you. I wanted to be here for you."

"I'm sorry that I pressured you, Charlie. Please don't do this to me again. This week was one of the worst of my life," I plead with her.

"Me, too. I'm sorry I put us both through it. But it made me realize that I do love you. I want to give us a chance, Brody. That is, if you still want me," she says to me shyly.

Bending down, I press my lips to hers. "I love you, honey – forever won't be long enough. Let's go." I grab her hand and pull her to the door she just came through.

She tugs on my hand. "Brody, we can't leave. This is your opening."

"They've got this. I want you, in my bed, where you belong," I tell her and pull her through the door. I don't give her the option. I take her to my SUV and put her in the front seat and then hold her hand the whole way to my home.

6

CHARLIE

Brody doesn't waste any time getting me into his car and to his house. After the week I've been through, I can't complain. I missed him way more than I thought I would. I couldn't focus on anything, because all I could think about was him. I kept going back to what Carrie said. I can't imagine my life without him. It took me a week to come to my senses, but I finally figured it out.

He's pulling me from the car and throws me over his shoulder. I laugh, smacking him on his ass. "Brody!" I scream indignantly.

But he doesn't stop moving until he has me in his bedroom and tosses me onto the bed.

He was laughing only moments ago, but when I look at him now, it's no laughing matter. He is about to ravage me. His eyes are dark with desire and his jaw is clenched tightly.

I back up on the bed to scoot away from him, but he grasps my ankle. "Oh no, honey. There's no stopping me now. You are mine."

He makes quick work of pulling off my clothes until I'm fully bared to him. I have one hand trying to cover my breast and the other cupping my pussy.

He pulls his shirt over his head and I can't take my eyes off the ripped muscles of his chest. My mouth is watering and I follow his hands as he pulls his dress pants and underwear down his thick, corded thighs. His cock springs up once it's free of the restraints, and my mouth falls open.

He is thick and long... and it's pointing right at me. His desire for me is evident in the precum already leaking from his tip. He moans and wraps his hand around himself, giving it a good stroke from root to tip. Getting up on my hands and knees, I forget to be modest and put my ass up in the air as I stroke his length with my tongue.

He hisses and sucks in a breath as I take him in as deeply as I can until he's hitting the back of my throat. Grabbing my hair, he holds me still as he pounds into my mouth. I moan around him, and he jerks back from me. Surprised, I look up at him and the look of determination on his face sets me on fire.

He pushes me until I'm lying on my back, my legs spread wide with his shoulders holding them open. He leans in and takes a big breath.

"You smell sweet as honey. I wake up with my hand around my cock every morning after dreaming of you," he tells me between kisses on my inner thighs. When he moves to my core and I feel his caress on my most private part, I moan his name.

His tongue does amazing things to me until my arms are thrashing on the bed and my legs tighten around his neck. When he rises up, he aligns himself at my entrance. "I want you to come on my cock, honey. I want to feel your sweet heat surround me."

"Yes, yes, Brody, please," I beg him.

He slowly enters me. "Uh, you're so tight, it feels so good." He moans while he's filling me up with his hard length.

He kisses up my stomach, and then sucks on my

nipple. I scream out as he bites down on me and my pussy explodes with heat. I'm fully stretched around him and he begins stroking in and out of me while my legs go up around his waist, pulling him in even deeper. "Oh, Brody, don't stop. Please don't stop."

Brody

"NEVER, HONEY, YOU'RE MINE," I moan as I thrust inside her. Her pussy vibrates around me and I try to hold back until she's about to come. But her pussy feels so good wrapped around me, almost like she's made for me.

With each thrust, I can feel her walls tighten on me until my cock feels like it's in a vice and I can barely thrust anymore.

"Come for me, baby. Milk my cock. Take all of me," I moan against her lips.

Her body flexes underneath me and she's grunting and moaning as she climaxes. I have to hold her hips down to let me move inside her, shooting my cum all over the walls of her channel. I don't stop until my balls are empty.

I pull out of her, lean over and kiss her on the lips. "I love you, Charlie."

"I love you, too," she whispers. She snuggles into my chest and I hold on to her with my arms and legs wrapped around her until we drift off to sleep.

EPILOGUE

BRODY

Two Months Later

PACING ON THE FRONT PORCH, I'm wondering where Charlie has gone.

She was sick this morning when I went in to work and I offered to stay home with her, but she insisted she was fine. Well, I ended up being able to call a manager in to come and cover for me so I rushed back home. To my surprise, Charlie was not there.

Picking up the phone, I dial her number.

When she answers on the first ring, I ask her, "Where are you? I came home to check on you and you're not here. Are you ..." I am in the middle of asking her if she's okay when I see her car pull into the driveway. I hit the button on my phone and walk over to help her out. She still doesn't look any better than she did this morning.

"I had to run to the store," she tells me as she grabs a paper bag out of the passenger seat.

"I could have gone for you. I'm sorry, honey. I never should have left you this morning," I tell her as I help her into the house.

She walks straight to the bedroom and sits down on the side of the bed. "There's something I need to tell you, Brody. I was going to wait until I knew for sure, but now that you are here, we probably need to talk about it."

"What is it?" I sit on the side of the bed next to her and pull the hair away from her face. "You're scaring me," I tell her when she doesn't look me in the face.

She still has a death grip on the paper bag and she opens it and reaches inside, pulling out a pink box. "I think I might be pregnant. We haven't been using anything and uh...well..."

I get down on my knees in front of her so she has to look at me. "I've told you that you are mine, sweetie. I have tried to tie you to me every way I know how. That's why I've asked you to marry me every day for the last two months. That's why I've come in you every night since then. I want you to be my wife and I want you to have my babies."

She smiles at me as tears start to fall down her face.

"Did you think I would be upset?" I ask her in amazement.

She hesitates. "I just didn't know... I wasn't sure."

"Well, honey, I'm one hundred percent sure. You are going to be my wife and the mother of my children. No matter what this pregnancy test says," I assure her as I start opening the box.

I crowd her in the bathroom until she insists she can't pee on a stick without me hovering over her. I wait until I hear the toilet flush before I barrel back into the room.

"Now, we just wait three minutes," she tells me.

EPILOGUE 2

CHARLIE

Two years and eight months later

TODAY IS our daughter Ashley's second birthday. Brody and I got married two weeks after we found out I was pregnant. I tried to convince him to put the wedding off until after our daughter was born, but he wasn't having it. He has turned into the absolute best dad. I think at first he was hoping for a boy. He about had a heart attack when we found out we were having a girl. He has gone into super protective mode.

Mike, Johnny, Ryder and Sierra are all here from my work. We also invited just a few kids from the play group too. There's one boy that keeps pulling Ashley's hair. Brody doesn't hesitate; he walks over and picks her up, bringing her back over to sit on his lap. I swear he gives the little boy a dirty look.

"You do know he's two, right?" I ask him.

"I protect what's mine, honey," he tells me possessively. "You know that."

Oh, I definitely know that. He's proven that to me over and over again.

"Daddy, down!" Ashley tells him that she wants to get down.

He looks over at the little boy and then finally lets her go, never taking his eyes off her. I laugh at how stressed out he is over one little boy. I decide to wait until tomorrow to tell him we are pregnant again.

THE END

HIS OBSESSION

1

MIKE

Another long day. I look over at Carrie with her body hovered over the computer, entering the last of the codes I need written. I think back to that day a year ago when I hired her. I was under pressure from Ryder, my partner, to hire someone capable – and someone I wouldn't hit on.

At first, I thought Carrie was the perfect person for the job. And one year later, she has proven herself more than capable. But my attraction for her these last few months has been something I haven't been able to control. And that bothers me. I'm used to being in control... in every situation.

I'm known as a player. I feel no need to turn down a beautiful woman. And why would I? If we are both into it and we both understand it's nothing serious –

then by all means, I plan to have my fun. But a night with Carrie – that's just a line I can't cross.

"Okay, I think that's it." Carrie sits up and stretches her back. Her arms come up over her head and her breasts press against her shirt. She finally took off her jacket an hour or so ago. I rarely see her without it. But looking at her now, it's probably good she's always wearing that ugly, boxy thing.

As she stretches her sore muscles, she moans and I can't stop my arousal. My cock presses tightly against the zipper of my pants. I don't know what's come over me lately. My extracurricular night life has slowed down. I'm just not interested anymore-not interested until I get around her.

Now I look for ways to spend more time at the office. And more often than not, I look for ways to have Carrie here with me.

Honestly, her boxy jackets and her hair in a knot on top of her head has started to grow on me.

But even if these new emotions are taking over – I know I can't make a move. I can't fuck this up. She really is the best assistant we've had. She was taking night classes in office management when she applied. And we took over paying for her classes – she's that good.

"I appreciate you staying again. I will quit taking advantage of you by making you work late all the time," I promise her.

A flush creeps across her cheeks. "I don't mind."

I lightly squeeze her shoulder. "Come on, I'll walk you out to your car."

She puts on her jacket and slings her purse over her shoulder. "You don't have to do that. I'm right by the door."

I put my hand at the small of her back because I can't seem to keep my hands to myself. "I know, but I will feel much better knowing you made it to your car safely."

When she drives away, my body is tense from being next to her all evening. I lock up the office and go to the pub across the street, needing to unwind before going home.

"What can I get you?" the waitress, Jasmine, asks me as she sits down on my leg. Instinctively, my hand slides around her hip and tightens around her tiny waist as her butt bone digs into my leg. This is a game we've played in the past. Yes, I've taken her home before. She was a good lay and she knew what the deal was. Just a night of fun. With her, I was able to get a release, without dealing with commitment or a relationship.

During the day, this pub is a place for business people to meet up and eat while working. And Jasmine is a perfect, professional waitress during the day. At night, it becomes a bar. And she becomes more forward. Six months ago, I would be sitting here picking which woman I wanted to take home with me. But tonight, like the last several months, I don't have any interest in taking her or any other woman home.

I help her up from my lap with a smile. "Jack and Coke."

She looks taken aback, but recovers quickly. "Be right back, Mike."

I'm forty-two years old and my fast lifestyle is finally catching up with me. I've had my share of women, but lately, it's not enough. Ryder and I opened our security company a few years ago and we haven't stopped since. We continue to grow every year, taking on more clients and more assignments, anything from security systems to personal protection with bodyguards.

I've watched Ryder find love and I have to admit I'm jealous. Watching him and Sierra together makes me realize what I don't have. And even my good friend Brody and one of our employees, Charlie found love with one another. I never thought I would see the day, but I'm ready to settle down. I'm ready for what they have.

Jasmine sets my drink down and takes the seat next to me. Her hand caresses my arm. "How about I come by your house after I get off?"

It's not even tempting to me. And plus, I never take women back to my house. I never want them to get the wrong idea.

"Sorry, not tonight." I pull my arm back gently. I smile at her to try and ease the turn-down. It's not her fault I'm not into it anymore- into her anymore.

I take a big swig of my drink and set it down with a loud clunk. Standing up, I throw a twenty on the table. "I'll see you around."

She stuffs the twenty into the apron at her waist and grabs my glass before walking away.

I walk away and go home – alone.

Carrie

"REMIND me again why you can't go?" I ask Charlie the next afternoon.

"Because this baby is doing a number on my stomach. I'm nauseated more often than not," she tells me as she pulls clothes off the rack.

I take an opportunity and look at her, really look at her, but all I see is a woman that is pregnant and shining with radiance.

"Okay. But that doesn't explain why Mike can't just go to this fundraiser by himself." I shake my head side to side at her when she pulls out a hot pink dress and holds it up to me.

She huffs, clearly over my efforts to get out of going tonight. "Look, Carrie, it was my idea for the company to donate to the women's care center. I should be there tonight for the fundraiser to present the check with Mike. But there's just no way I can do it. I can't go there and barf all over everyone. All you have to do is show up with the check, give it to Mike and he will present it. You just stand next to him and look beautiful."

Snorting, I cover my face to try and hide my giggles. Catching myself in the mirror, I look down at my black dress pants and a boxy jacket over a loose-fitting black shirt. Beautiful? I don't think so. I'm curvier than most. I know I don't dress right. My dad was a single father and I never had a mom or mother figure in my life. I never had clothes that fit me. All I ever had were hand-me-downs from my brother. I never wore makeup— hell, I've never even bought it. I was raised working on cars and as I look down at my chipped nails, I shrug my shoulders. I know I'm a lost cause.

Turning away from the mirror, I follow Charlie to the next clothes rack. "I can't do this. All I'm going to do is embarrass him and in turn embarrass myself. I mean, look at me. He is not going to be happy that I'm just showing up like this."

She hangs up the clothes, comes over to me and grabs both of my hands. "Do you trust me?"

"What – of course." I shrug at her. If nothing else, Charlie has proven herself trustworthy. She's always been pretty quiet around me, but ever since I talked to her one day when she was upset about Brody, she has really opened up to me.

"I would never put you in a situation that I think is going to be bad. Give me the next few hours and I will have you ready for tonight. No one, not even Mike, will be upset or embarrassed that you showed up."

"I just don't know – " I start, until she swats at me.

"Trust me. I promise you it will work out. You are beautiful, honey. I'm just going to help you realize it."

Looking into her eyes, I see the sincerity in them and I want so badly to trust her. Putting my complete faith in her, I nod my head. "Okay, make me beautiful then. Or as close to it as you can."

We spend the next few hours shopping for a dress and shoes. She even convinces me to buy some new clothes for work that actually fit me. We went shoe shopping, bought makeup, and then she leads me into the salon.

"I'm not cutting my hair," I tell her without hesitation.

Holding her hands up in front of her, she says, "I

know that. First we are going to take it out of this bun. I swear I've never seen your hair down." She unknots it from the top of my head and it falls down around my shoulders, reaching almost to my butt.

"Oh my God, it's beautiful." She stares at me, looking startled. "Why would you wear this up all the time?"

I shrug. "I don't know how to fix it."

She grasps my hand and pulls me toward her friend that is waiting on us. "Well, she is going to show you."

I leave the salon with a new do. She trimmed my hair, shaped it and thinned it out a little. She even showed me how to fix it straight or curly. I left there with products and curling irons and straightening irons. I even got my nails and toenails done.

When we get back to my house, my dad is still at work. Thank goodness. I don't know if he's ready to see his little girl like this. I mean, I'm twenty years old, but he's used to seeing me - well, not like this.

Charlie does my makeup. She won't let me look in the mirror until she's done. She brings me my new dress, a form-fitting A-line in a royal blue. She says it brings out the color of my eyes.

When I'm dressed and ready to go, she stands back and looks at her handiwork. She is looking at me in awe and I swear my stomach is turning somersaults, nervous about seeing myself.

She grabs my shoulders. "Don't freak out."

I feel like I'm going to be sick. She turns me around to face the mirror. My mouth falls open and all I can do is stare. I turn my head side to side, looking at myself like I'm seeing me for the very first time.

"I'm beautiful," I stutter.

Charlie's grinning ear to ear at me in the mirror. "I told you so."

2

MIKE

Looking at the time on my phone, I drop it back into my pants pocket. Well, she's late. Charlie talked me into coming to this fundraiser and now she's late. Not that I mind being here, it really is for a good cause, but I can do without the whole black tie and jacket.

Tugging at my collar, I look around the room again. Still no sight of Charlie. We have fifteen minutes until the check dedications start and I don't have the check because she said she would bring it with her. Grabbing my phone again, I decide to give her a call. Honestly, I'm surprised her husband was going to let her come to this thing with me. We are good friends, but he's pretty possessive of her.

"Sorry I'm late."

I look up from my phone, gasp and drop it to the floor. *Oh my God.* "Carrie?"

"Yes, sorry, I know you were expecting Charlie, but she wasn't feeling well. She had me bring the check to you," she says as she's bending down to pick up my phone from the ground. When she stands back up, I can't take my eyes off her exposed cleavage.

"You, uh, you look beautiful," I stutter.

She blushes a pretty shade of red and it spreads across her chest. I can't believe this is Carrie. She has worked for us the past year. She's funny and dedicated to her job. She's extremely efficient and honestly I don't know what we would do without her sometimes. But now I can add absolutely beautiful to her list of attributes. How in the world has she been hiding these curves under those boxy jackets? Why has she?

I finally raise my eyes to her face. "What happened?"

Smiling back at me, she says, "Oh, uh, I think she has been nauseous..."

"No, not what happened with Charlie. What happened with you?" I ask her as I grab her hand and walk her over to the side of the room, somewhere more private.

She nervously wraps her fingers around the clutch in her hands. Her bright blue eyes are wide staring back at me and my first instinct is to kiss the pink lipstick off her lips. "Charlie helped me go shopping."

I brush the hair off her face. "Well, you look beautiful."

"Thank you." Reaching into her clutch, she pulls out the check. "They are getting started. Here's the check."

"Huh, what?" Did I miss the announcement?

"Go on up there." She waves toward the stage.

I lace her fingers with mine. "Oh, you are going with me." And then I mutter to myself, *I'm not letting you out of my sight*.

Carrie

HE HOLDS my hand all the way up the stage. When they introduce him, we go to the podium with my hand still wrapped around his.

"On behalf of Alpha Security, we would like to present this check of thirty thousand dollars to the

Women's Care Center. We also want to thank you for everything you do for the women and children in our community..."

As he continues his speech, I can't help but look at him in awe. I've been in love with Mike since the day he interviewed me. He's tall, handsome and confident. He's a good man. Even after working for him this past year, I still haven't been able to find any fault with him.

I realize as he's speaking, his thumb is stroking my hand and I can't stop myself from looking down at my hand in his. The audience laughs and it jolts me from my trance. When I look back up at him, he's looking at me and I gasp at the heat I see in his eyes.

I want to think it's for me, but I'm not so sure. Mike has been known to be a player... He dates plenty of women. Surely, he wouldn't treat me as just another notch on his bedpost.

The rest of the night flies by. We dance a few times and when the DJ changes the music to a slow song, I get nervous and excuse myself to the ladies' room. I don't think I could handle being that close to him and being held in his arms. He hasn't left my side the whole night and when I come out he is standing by the door waiting on me.

I try not to blush when I see him, which is hard to do. I'm sure I've been red all night. "Well, I think I need to go home. It's getting late," I say and walk past him.

He grabs my hand. "Can I take you home?"

I shake my head, but I still can't bring myself to look at him. I'm worried if I do, I will throw myself at him. "No, that's okay. I drove here."

Still holding my hand, he walks with me to the front door. He waves at a few people that are still here, but he doesn't stop. "Where are you parked?"

I point over to the corner parking lot and he walks me toward it.

When we reach my car, I unlock it and he opens the door for me, standing back to let me in.

Before I get in, I thank him for a great night.

He leans in and kisses me on the cheek. "I'm glad you came, Carrie."

I gasp as his lips touch me and my hand instinctively goes to my cheek where his lips were. I slide into my seat and he shuts the door. When I pull out, I look in the rearview mirror, and he's standing in the same spot watching me drive away.

3

MIKE

I WALK in to work an hour late the next morning. This is the first time I've ever been late. I tried and tried to fall asleep but I couldn't get the image of Carrie out of my head. Carrie in her form-fitting dress showing off her ample curves. I eventually had to stroke my cock to make it go down. Cold showers just were not doing it.

All I can think about is Carrie. How could she have been right under my nose all this time and I didn't realize it? I knew she was funny. Heck, I know everything about her. But how did I miss knowing that she was drop dead gorgeous?

When I walk through the front door, it barely shuts before I'm looking straight at the person that caused me to have a sleepless night.

Carrie rises from her desk. Her blond hair, which is usually in a bun, is lying in big curls down her shoulders. She has on a tight-fitting blue shirt that shows off her curves and black pants. I look around for the boxy jacket, wishing I could cover her up and hide her from the rest of the world.

"Here you go." She walks over and hands me a small stack of messages. Every day. She has done the same thing every day for the last year and I usually just take them, thank her and walk away.

My cock stiffens in my pants and I mutter *thank you* and walk into my office. My reaction to her is fierce and I don't know if I can control it being this close to her.

I barely sit down before there is a knock on my door. Excitement surges through me that it could be Carrie. But in a way, I hope it's not. There's only so much temptation I can take and I really need to get myself together before I see her next.

"Come in," I holler.

Charlie walks in. "Hey, Mike, I'm really sorry about last night."

Pointing, I ask her, "Can you shut the door please?"

She looks back at me surprised but does as I ask.

Accusingly, I ask her, "What did you do?"

Her nose squinches up. "What do you mean? I didn't do anything."

Frustrated, I throw my hands in the air. "I mean with Carrie. What did you do to Carrie?"

She giggles. "I know, right? She's a bombshell, isn't she?"

Nodding, I have to agree. She is beautiful.

"But why? I don't get it," I question her again. I just want to understand.

Her shoulders lift as she takes a deep breath. "Look, I owed her. She really helped me out once when I was having a personal problem and so I thought this would be perfect. She's been talking about wanting a boyfriend and I knew no one would give her a second glance in those boxy clothes she always wears."

My brain stopped working after she said the word boyfriend. "What do you mean she wants a boyfriend?"

She startles at my question. "Well... I guess she's

never had one. She's even enlisted Johnny to give her 'dating' lessons." And when she uses finger quotes when she says 'dating,' my whole body tightens up and she gasps at the look on my face.

My hands wrap around the corner of my desk and my knuckles go white. The thought of Johnny anywhere near her makes me want to hurl my computer off the desk. "Okay, that will be all," I tell her shortly.

"Look, if what I did interferes with her job – which I don't see how it could – but if it does, I'm sorry. She had been down on herself and I knew I could help her. I ..."

Interrupting her, I open the door for her. "No, I'm glad you helped her. Nothing is going to interfere with her job."

She looks at me for a minute and I swear I see mischief in her eyes. But she shrugs her shoulders and walks out the door.

Carrie

THE DAY HAS GONE BY SLOWLY and I

blame it on the fact that Mike has not been out of his office at all today. I almost work up enough nerve to go and check on him when the pager on my desk buzzes. "Carrie, can you come in here?"

I grab my pad and pen and walk into his office.

He walks around his desk and leans against it. "Have a seat."

I sit in a chair and he's standing right in front of me with his pelvis right in front of me. I can't stop myself from looking at him appreciatively.

When he clears his throat, I look up at him and then quickly look down at the pad of paper in my lap, as if I'm ready to start taking notes.

"I'm ready, sir." He gasps when I say it. I don't know why I did. I've always called him Mike, but today, I called him sir. His nostrils flare and I can't tell by his look if I've ticked him off or well, what that look means. "I mean, Mike."

He sits down at the chair next to me. "So, I don't know how else to do it but just say it."

Instantly, my heart sinks. I press my palm to my chest. He's firing me.

He rushes out in one breath, "I don't want Johnny to give you dating lessons."

My mouth falls open. "How did you know? Did Johnny tell you?"

He puts his hand on mine that is still holding the pen. "No. Charlie told me, but only because I pressured her to. Please don't be mad at her."

Struggling to get ahold of my thoughts, I jump up from my seat. "This is so embarrassing." I drag my hands down my face to cover it and take a deep breath. "Of course, of course, it was inappropriate for me to ask him. I...I..."

"Carrie, stop." He grabs my arms and pulls me back to the chair I just jumped up from. "Sit down," he orders me.

I sit down but I can't bring myself to look up at him.

Squatting down, he pushes the hair back from my face. "I just don't think it's a good idea... for you two to date and work together."

"No. Of course not. We aren't dating. We are friends. I got to talking one day and just mentioned that I never had been on a date and wouldn't know what to do. I asked him if he would help me. But of course, you're right. It's not a good idea. I will tell him."

I brush at the tears rolling down my face and try to look away from him.

He holds onto each of my shoulders and grips them tightly. "Honey, stop, don't cry. Why are you crying?"

I try to get myself together and try to pull away from him. "Nothing. Nothing. I'm fine."

He tilts his head to the side. "Why do you feel like you need lessons?"

Fidgeting and squirming in my seat, I look everywhere but at him. "Well, I uh, well – no one has ever asked me out and I think I should know how to act is all. I was raised by a single dad and stuff that is normal to other people – I'm finding out – is not normal to me."

He furrows his brow and tightens his fist on my shoulders. "I'll do it."

Squeezing my eyes shut, I don't think this can get any more embarrassing. I shrug out of his grasp and stand up, almost knocking him to the ground.

Walking to the door, I don't stop until he grabs my hand to stop me. "I said I'll do it."

I draw a breath and release it. "No, that doesn't make sense. You're my boss. Why would you want to help me?"

He winks at me. "You should learn from the best."

He catches me by surprise and I bust out laughing. I can always depend on Mike to smooth out an embarrassing situation. "I'm sorry I tried to involve someone at work with my personal life. It won't happen again."

He pulls my hand he's still holding up between us. "I want to do it. I don't trust anyone else to do it. I won't have you taken advantage of."

"Johnny wouldn't ..." I start to say until he interrupts me.

"I know that. I trust Johnny, but I just want to do this myself. Don't you trust me?"

Swaying back and forth, which is something I do when I'm nervous, I tell him, "Yes, of course I do, but I can't ask you - my boss - to do this."

He starts shaking his head before I even finish the sentence. "You're not asking me... I'm telling you. I want to do it. Now, that's it. We both have work to do. I will pick you up at six tonight."

I stare in awe at him until I get the courage to speak. "Uh, okay. Uh I can just meet you..."

"It's a date, Carrie. I'll pick you up."

4

MIKE

THE REST of the day went so slow, I thought it would never end. Standing outside Carrie's house, I ring the doorbell.

"Hey, Mr. Masters. Come on in, Carrie will be down in a minute." I shake his hand firmly and the age difference between Carrie and myself smacks me in the face. I'm only a few years younger than her father and I have to wonder how he feels about me taking his daughter out.

"How have you been, Mr. Smith?" I ask him politely.

"Good. Good. I want to thank you for taking my girl out for a work thing tonight. I'm afraid she never gets to go out and she's been pretty excited about it." He slaps me on the shoulder as he says it.

So this is how she handled it. She didn't tell her dad it was a date, she told him it was a work thing. I guess that will have to do for now.

"Of course. She has been a Godsend in the office. We couldn't make it without her."

Thumping on the stairwell has me turning toward it. Carrie is walking down the stairs and she looks amazing. She has on a skirt that comes to her knees and a white blouse. Her long blond hair is pulled up in a ponytail and it sways with each step she takes.

"Hey, Mike." She purrs my name. Turning to her dad, she says, "I love you, Dad. I will be back..."

"Ha ha, Kitten. No worries. You are with Mr. Masters. I trust him to get you home safe." He gives me a smile and matter-of-fact look over her head and all I can do is nod at him.

I help her into my SUV and when I get into the driver's seat, I ask her, "So we are doing a work thing?"

She smiles at me with a sad smirk on her face. "Well, I didn't think you would want people to know exactly what you are helping me with, so I thought that was the best thing to say. Which I hate, because I've never lied to my dad before. I feel sort of guilty."

"You don't have to lie. Just tell him we are dating, honey. It's not a lie," I assure her.

"But you don't date," she blurts out and then covers her mouth with her hands. Her eyes are wide, staring back at me.

"I don't date. Usually. I guess I do now," I announce to her and pull out into traffic.

My plans are to keep my hands to myself the whole evening. But I don't know how long that will last. When I saw her walking down the steps, all I could imagine was lifting her skirt up over her head and showing her exactly what I want to do with her. I had to fight with myself to calm my erection. Imagine having to explain that to her dad. She's right, I don't date. But for her, I want to start.

I take her to a new Italian restaurant that opened a few weeks ago. I wanted to take her somewhere that she hadn't been before. After we order, we talk about work until I ask her to tell me about her.

"You already know all about me," she assures me.

"Well, tell me something I don't know." I reach over and hold her hand across the table.

She looks down at our hands and I interrupt her

thoughts. "When you are on a date, a man is going to want to always be touching you. If you want them to, you let them. If you don't, you pull your hand from theirs and tell them so."

She smiles at me and her hand curls into mine. I release a breath I didn't know I was holding.

"I like to read romance novels. It's probably ruined me on men in real life," she confesses.

"You deserve romance. Don't settle," I tell her as the waitress sets our food down in front of us. I keep holding her hand, just because I want to be touching her.

"Tell me something about you. Something nobody knows," she asks me.

"Well, you know everything there is to know about me," I assure her.

"C'mon, Mike, there has to be something." She smiles mischievously, like I'm about to tell her a big secret.

"Okay, uh, I haven't been out with a woman in around six months."

She gasps and her fork makes a loud noise when she drops it in her plate. Her mouth hanging open, she says, "What? Why? No way."

I think about it and try to find the right words. "I just haven't been interested. I feel like I'm at the age now where I need to start thinking about settling down."

She's staring at me with her eyes wide. I swear I see hope in her eyes, but just as quickly, it disappears.

She clears her throat. "Uh, you act like you're ancient. You're forty-two years old."

"I know how old I am, honey. Just like I know how old you are." I say it out loud because I have to remind myself that she's only twenty and not only that, but an inexperienced twenty-year-old.

We go through the rest of the meal and I try to slow it down. I don't want the night to end. Not yet anyway.

"So, you are doing great on your first date," I compliment her.

She turns red, like I knew she would. Shrugging her shoulders, she says, "Thanks. But it's easy with you. Plus, I don't feel as nervous because I know this isn't a real date."

I pull my hand away from her. Damn. Of course she doesn't think this is a real date. What have I gotten myself into? I finally find someone I want to date, and I can't. She's my employee and she's too young.

I stand up and throw some bills on the table. "You ready to go?"

She lifts the napkin from her lap and puts it on the table. "Yes, sure."

I grab her hand and walk her to the car.

———

Carrie

EVERYTHING WAS GOING SO WELL, but now it's like he can't get away from me fast enough. The ride back to my house is quiet and I can't help but wonder if I did something wrong.

I try to break the silence, but he answers me and then turns his attention back to the road. When he pulls into the driveway, I tell him thank you and start walking toward my house.

"Wait, honey. You always let your date walk you to the door. Unless it was a bad one, then you can leave him at the restaurant or in the car."

I nod and slow my steps. "Well, I do appreciate you taking me out, Mike. I had a really good time."

He looks surprised and like he's struggling with something, but tells me, "Yes, me too."

I put my key in the door. "Well, I'll see you..."

He presses against me and whispers, "Usually if you have had a good date, it ends with a goodnight kiss."

I gasp and turn around. My breasts are pressed against his chest. He didn't move back when I whirled around; if anything, he got even closer.

"Do you want to kiss me?" I ask him and then fiddle with the hem of my shirt nervously.

His hands go to my shoulders and hold me close. "Yes. More than anything. Even though I'm over twenty years older than you and I'm your boss. I still want to kiss you."

I close my eyes and start to lean in. He meets me halfway and when his lips touch mine I have to hold in my gasp of pleasure. His lips are warm, strong and firm. He moves them against mine and this time, I let out a soft moan, giving him access for his tongue to touch against mine. The kiss is over in almost seconds and when he pulls away from me, he rests his forehead against mine.

"Goodnight, sweetie. I'll see you in the morning." He kisses my forehead and walks away. The warmth I felt in his arms is gone and now I'm chilled in the night air by myself. Touching my fingers to my lips and feeling their warmth, I go inside and relive the night in my dreams.

5
———

MIKE

ANOTHER SLEEPLESS NIGHT has my nerves shot. I walk into the office early the next morning, so early that I'm the first one here. I go in and shut the door, not coming out until lunchtime.

"Hey, Carrie, I'm going to be out of the office this afternoon, but I'll be back later. Do you care to work a little late this evening?"

She blushes a pretty red and I have to stop myself from crossing the room and holding her in my arms. "Of course," she tells me with a smile.

The afternoon flies by and when I get back, we go to a conference room to work. I have her draft a few letters and take some notes of things that need to be completed for the week. After we finish working, I ask her, "You ready for date number two?"

"Sure, what do you have in mind? Do I look okay?" She gestures down at her black dress and jean jacket.

I help her up from her chair and put a small kiss on the end of her nose. "You look perfect. I thought we would just go across the street and grab a bite to eat at the pub."

"Sounds good. Let me grab my purse."

When we walk in, I ask for a booth in the corner. The restaurant is dark and it looks like everyone is stopping in after a long day of work, wanting to unwind. We are looking at the menu when Jasmine comes over and sits beside me in the booth. "Long time no see, honey. How have you been?" Her hand strokes up and down my arm and I instantly grit my teeth. I'm embarrassed that this is happening in front of Carrie. Her eyes are huge, staring at me and then at Jasmine, and then at her hand on my arm.

I pull it away from her. "Honey, what would you like to eat?"

She folds the menu and sets it down on the table. "Just a salad would be fine."

I grit my teeth because I know she's comparing herself to Jasmine and that's the last thing she should be doing. Her curvy body is what every one of my dreams are made of.

I hand the menus to Jasmine and order our food, but never take my eyes off of Carrie. "She will have the filet, with a baked potato and a salad. I will have the same. Thanks."

She is still looking between me and Jasmine and I don't want her to. I want her eyes on me. When Jasmine walks away with a huff, Carrie looks bewildered. "I think she likes you."

"She does. But I'm on a date with you," I tell her.

"Oh, well you, uh, I mean, I don't want to mess up anything between you and her," she says shyly.

"There is no me and her. I'm here with you, because that's where I want to be. There are going to be times where women hit on me. And there will be times that men hit on you, God help them. But I'm going to help you here with this, since I'm supposed to be giving you lessons. If you are out with me and another woman touches me, I don't want her to. The only hands I want on me are yours, honey."

"Really?" she asks me hesitantly.

"Really," I tell her matter-of-factly.

She looks straight at me like she's trying to see how sincere I am. "Can I come over there and sit next to you?"

I slide farther into the booth. "Absolutely."

When she slides in next to me, her skirt slides up her thighs. Confidently, she grabs my hand and puts it on her bare thigh. I stroke my finger along her soft skin and my cock about explodes in my pants. I shift in my seat to try and get more comfortable.

When Jasmine brings our food to the table, she sets it down in front of us and walks away. We eat in comfortable silence. Luckily, the steaks are tender and I'm able to cut it with my fork. Because my hand is not leaving her thigh. After we finish eating she's telling me stories about her college class and her funny instructor. She turns to me, excited, and as she comes closer, my hand slides up her thigh and my fingers graze the edge of her panty covered pussy. We both freeze.

I start to pull away. "I'm sorry..."

"No," she moans into my ear. "Don't stop." And she scoots even closer to me.

"Honey, are you sure?" I ask her hesitantly, but even as I'm waiting on her to answer, I slide my finger along the damp cloth over her lips.

"Yes," she moans.

I pull her panties to the side and slide my finger through her soaked core.

"Oh, baby, you are so wet," I tell her as I stroke back and forth.

"I know. I'm always like this when I'm around you. Every day. Even at work," she admits.

The image of bending her over her desk while I push my cock deep into her folds about makes me come in my pants. I'll never be able to work now, knowing that she's wet like this for me.

"Has anyone ever touched you like this before?" I think I know the answer, but I have to ask her anyway.

"Nobody. Never." She moans when I push even deeper inside her. Her back is to the rest of the dark restaurant and I wish I was sitting on the outside so I could shield her body from everyone.

My nostrils flare with the essence of her arousal filling the booth. "I wish we were somewhere else.

Anywhere else because I want to put my mouth on you and taste you."

I stroke my hand along her clit and she starts gyrating her hips against me, moaning my name. I kiss her then, because I can't hold back. I pull back enough to tell her to be quiet, that I don't want anyone to hear her when she comes. She kisses me back and when she's totally gone, ecstasy taking over, her head slides down to my shoulder. I put more pressure on her swelled clit until she's biting down on me to keep from screaming her release. When her body freezes and tightens up, I don't stop. I don't stop until I know she's leaking her cum all over my hand.

I cup her jaw and kiss her deeply. "Fuck, honey, that was hot."

She smiles at me and it makes me even hotter for her. I pull my hand from between her legs. I lick my finger that was just inside her and moan as her taste explodes on my tongue. She tastes so good.

Carrie

I DON'T KNOW what's happening to me. I'm not

the girl that has an orgasm in a booth at a restaurant. I would never do that. At least, I never thought I would do that. Mike just does something to me. He brings out this lust-filled woman in me that wants to push myself to the edge every day.

After our action at the restaurant, he walked me to my car and kissed me goodnight. I didn't want the night to end, but I didn't know how to tell him that. I think he's taking it slow with me and I sort of appreciate it. If I end up being just another notch on his bedpost, I don't think I would survive it. But honestly, I think he's trying to do right by me.

The next morning, he smiles at me when he comes in but then he stows himself in his office most of the morning. I think about trying to talk to him. We aren't really hiding anything, but I doubt he wants the whole office to know he's dating an employee.

I had forgotten that I promised to go to lunch with Johnny so when he comes by my desk, I grab my purse. I think about telling Mike, but I see he's on the phone so I don't bother him.

Lunch with Johnny is always a treat. He is so different from anyone I've ever met. He's covered in tattoos and a little rough around the edges. But he is also one of the sweetest men I've ever met. I've heard that he's had a hard life, but I've never been privy to the details. I do know he is handsome. And I'm surprised he doesn't have a girlfriend. So I ask him about it.

He's stuffing a hamburger in his mouth and almost chokes on it at my question. "Uh, I just don't want one."

"Whatever, Johnny. I've seen you watching Ryder and Sierra. You want what they have. Why don't you go for it?"

He looks at me and for a second I think he's going to answer my question, but then he turns the tables on me. "So how are your lessons going? I saw you walk into the pub last night."

My whole body heats up when he asks me that. I just smirk at him. "Fine. I get it. You don't want to talk about it. Neither do I."

We both laugh and start talking about work.

As we are walking back to the office, Johnny says, "Hey, heads up. Charlie has been scoping out a date for you. I figured since you haven't told her you were dating boss man that I would stay out of it. But you may want to talk to her. He doesn't seem the type to want to share."

I just laugh at him. Honestly, how is this my life? A few days ago, a man would never even look at me. Now I am dating my boss and a friend is lining me up with dates. Not that I plan on going on any, but it does feel nice to be wanted.

6

MIKE

At lunch time, I walk out of my office hoping to take Carrie to grab a bite to eat. I haven't gotten to see her most of the morning because I've been super busy, but I hope to remedy that. When she's not at her desk, I see Charlie by the water cooler. "Hey, have you seen Carrie?"

"Yes, she went to lunch with Johnny," she tells me before taking a big chug of water.

My fists clench at my sides. Charlie doesn't notice, because she continues, "I really think her new look has helped her confidence. She has been absolutely glowing here lately. I talked to one of Brody's friends and I think he will be perfect for her. A double date is just the ticket."

Still clueless, she throws her cup in the trash and keeps walking, never noticing that my face is, I'm sure, white as a ghost.

When I hear Carrie come in from lunch, I busy myself on the computer.

She lays a brown bag on my desk and the smell of hamburger fills my nostrils. My stomach growls, because I haven't eaten anything today.

"Thank you," I say and then, because I can't stop myself, I add, "How was your lunch?"

"It was good. I was going to tell you where I was going but you were on the phone when I left," she explains.

I raise my hand to stop her. "You don't owe me an explanation. I don't need to know where you've been. Thanks for the lunch but I have to get back to work."

I see the hurt on her face and I almost take the words back. What I really wanted to tell her was she's not permitted to date anyone else or go out to lunch with someone else, but I don't.

When she walks out of my office, I slump over my desk. What am I doing? I ask myself. I want her. I'm pretty sure she wants me. So why am I pushing her away? But instantly I think about how young and inexperienced she is. She just found her confidence. I can't strap her down to me knowing that I don't plan on letting her go. It's better for her to get experience, no matter how badly it hurts.

I avoid her the next two weeks. I see her every day, and I treat her just like I did before we went out on our date. I can see the tiredness in her eyes and I have to wonder if she's sleeping okay. I know I'm not. But of course, it could be because she's dating Charlie's friend now and is getting home late.

The thought of her with someone else almost has me doubled over in pain. So many times, I almost pull her to me and ravage her lips… but I don't.

On Friday the following week, I walk out of my office and her chair is empty. It looks like she has already left for the day. I look at my watch and realize it's after five. But still, she usually tells me bye before she leaves.

Johnny is walking from the back and notices me standing there, staring at her chair. "She already left. Charlie said she had a date tonight."

My fists clench and I stride back into my office and slam the door.

Seconds go by and Johnny follows me in. "Look, I don't know what's happened between the two of you but you better grow some balls or you are going lose her forever."

Enraged, I'm standing chest to chest to him and I'm not backing down. But neither is he. "Mike, you have both been miserable these past two weeks. Don't you see what you are doing to her?"

I throw my hands up. "What do you care? I thought you wanted her anyway."

"We are friends. That's it. She thinks you didn't want anyone to know you were dating. And no, she didn't tell me. I saw you together one night at the pub across the street. And she never told Charlie about you and her, so she has pretty much forced her into going on this date tonight."

My hands clench and unclench at my sides as I try to wrap my head around it all. Could I still have a chance with her – or did I totally fuck this up?

"Where did she go?" I ask him as I grab my keys.

"I don't know, but he picked her up here and I would guess her car is still outside. She'll be back."

I sit down at my desk and put my head in my hands. *Oh Carrie, what have I done?*

When Johnny starts to walk out, I call out to him, "Thanks, brother."

He just smiles back at me. "No problem. But try not to fuck this up."

I sit here for what seems like hours, watching the security camera, not taking my eyes off her car. When I see a car pull in next to hers, I jump out of my seat, stride out the side of the office, and stand in the shadows.

Carrie

WELL, that was a mess. I knew before I even met him that this wouldn't go well. He took me to a pizza place down the road. The food was good, but the whole time all I thought about was Mike. Which wasn't fair to my date, Brent.

I think he finally got tired of trying to bring me into

conversation and just drove me back to my car. I apologized to him for my behavior and explained that I had been hurt recently and just hadn't gotten over it. He accepted my apology. When he dropped me off at my car, he didn't even wait until I got in before he drove off. I can't say I blame him.

I don't even realize that Mike is standing there until he comes out of the shadows. "You didn't kiss him goodnight."

I smile at him, but then remember the last two weeks and the pain I've felt. "Nope." I get into my car. "I'll see you tomorrow."

He puts his hand on the door to stop me from closing it. "Can we talk?"

I lean my head against the steering wheel. I've been a basket of emotions this whole week and I know I'm on the verge of crying. "Can we talk in the morning?" I ask him without lifting my head.

"If it's okay with you, I'd rather talk tonight."

"Well, you're the boss, so let's talk," I tell him and jump out of my seat, pushing him back in the process and then slam my car door. "Where do you want to talk? Inside? If you're firing me, just do it."

He leans down to where I'm looking him right in the face. "Fire you? I could never fire you. C'mon, Carrie, I know you're mad and you have a right to be. But please just give me a few minutes."

I nod and follow him into the office.

" Have a seat," he tells me, pointing at his chair behind his desk.

I look at him questioningly, but he pulls the seat out for me.

"Do you remember six months ago when I asked you to order me an extra monitor for the cameras?"

I do remember that day. I didn't understand why he needed an extra one, but I never questioned him on it. "Yes," I mutter.

"That's it right there." He points to a monitor on the corner of his desk. It's by itself, away from the computer monitor and other camera monitor. "Turn it on."

I lean forward and hit the button to turn the screen on. The screen is black only momentarily before it lights up with an image of my empty desk.

Gasping, I exclaim, "I don't understand. What is this?"

"Around six months ago, I started having feelings for you. I couldn't get you out of my head. Even with your hair in a knot on your head or that boxy jacket you always wore. All I thought about was you. I had my eyes on you all day, every day. I knew then that I wanted you. But when you had your little makeover, you brought out a fierce possessive side of me that I couldn't tame."

I reach for his hand and he laces his fingers with mine. "Oh, Mike, I..."

But he interrupts me. "I need to get this out. When I found out how inexperienced you were I knew that I had to give you time to date and meet other men. No matter how much it killed me. I needed to know for sure I was the one you wanted. Because there's no going back, honey."

She slaps me on the hand. "Is this what this has been? You were testing me... Do you know what I've been through these last two weeks? I wish you had trusted me, because my opinion hasn't changed. I choose you. I will always choose you."

He smiles at me before leaning in and pressing his lips to mine. "I'm so sorry, honey. These past two weeks have killed me and knowing you were out with another man tonight about put me over the edge."

He pulls me up from the chair and sits me down on his desk, muscling his body between my legs so that my skirt rides up my hips.

His hands slide up my thighs as he kisses me over and over, showing me exactly how much he has missed me.

Pulling back from him, I say, "Never again, Mike. You can never push me away again. If this is going to work, you have to talk to me."

He kisses my neck. "I promise you we are going to work. You are stuck with me now. I'm never walking away from you again."

I'm so desperate to feel him against me, I tug my shirt over my head and my skirt up my hips.

"Oh, God, you're beautiful," he says huskily and then latches his lips on to the cloth covering my nipple. With one hand he unclasps my bra and pulls it from my body.

My breasts are loose and my nipples are hard, seeking his attention. He moves from one to the other, lavishing each with his tongue until I'm about to lose my mind.

I tug off his shirt and his muscles flex under my hands. I rub the hardness of his chest and along his taut abs. Leaning over, I lick one of his nipples and he moans my name. Encouraged by his moan, I unzip his pants and pull his pants and underwear down with one sweep of my hand. His long hard cock bounces up, pointing at me. He's leaking with precum and all I want to do is lean over and take him in my mouth.

He stops me by putting his hands on my shoulders. "Honey, I don't want your first time to be on my desk. Let me take you home."

"No, I need you, Mike. Please make me yours. I want you to take me on this desk so when you are working you always remember it. Then you can take me home."

He grips my thighs and pulls me to the edge. His cock strokes along my wet slit and I cream at the intensity of it.

He wraps his hand around his large shaft and lines it up at my entrance. "It's going to hurt for a minute, but I promise I will make it good for you."

I kiss his lips and smile at him. I'm not scared of the pain. I'm scared he's going to change his mind. "I know you will. Just do it. I want it... I want you."

He slowly enters me until his bulb is the only thing in me. Even with just that, I feel so full. I moan as he inches in even more and I press my nails into his shoulders, pulling him toward me.

"Please, don't stop. Don't stop," I beg him.

He moves even further inside of me until he rips through my hymen and bottoms out inside me with his balls pressed against my ass. "I couldn't stop if I tried. I'm going to fuck you and bury my seed deep inside your womb. No one will ever doubt you are taken. I'm going to mark you head to toe."

"Yes, Yes..." I scream as my hips instinctively start moving back and forth. The pain was over as quick as it started and all I feel now is an intensity that is forcing me to move my hips back and forth. With each stroke inside my channel, I cream all over him.

He rests his head against mine and his chest is slick with sweat. "Baby, I'm about to come. I need you to come so that I can fill you up. Come for me, baby. Milk me."

With each thrust, his pelvis grinds against my clit

until I'm screaming his name and clenching his cock. He's still pushing in and out of me, and I can't stop the contractions that are taking over my body.

When our breathing comes back to normal, he asks me if I'm okay.

"I've never felt better," I tell him honestly.

He pulls out of me and I see the remnants of my virginity coating his member. He pulls me from the desk and kisses me. "Get dressed, I'm taking you home."

EPILOGUE

CARRIE

I thought he was taking me to my home – or my dad's home. But that wasn't the case. He had me leave my car at the office and he drove me to his house.

"What am I going to tell my dad?" I ask him.

He kisses me on the cheek. "Send him a text and tell him you're with me. I'll talk to him tomorrow."

I look at him like he's talking crazy, but all he says is, "It's either that or I go over and talk to him tonight. You pick."

"Fine, I'll text him."

My phone dings, letting me know there's a response. *Ok. See you tomorrow. Love you.*

After I read him the text, I start laughing. " I can't believe that he's okay with me staying out all night with you. It doesn't make sense."

"I called him earlier. When I was waiting on you to get home from your date." His face pinches up when he says the word date.

"You called him? What did you say?"

He leans down and kisses me. "That I love his daughter and plan to marry her."

I gasp as he picks me up and swings me around. Laughingly, I ask him, "Don't you think you better ask me first?"

He carries me into the bedroom and tosses me to the bed. "Nope. You're marrying me, honey. You are going to be mine forever."

He follows me down until he's lying on top of me. I kiss him long and hard. "That's fine, but you're mine too."

"There's no doubt about that," he says as he begins to undress me again.

THE END

HIS REDEMPTION

1

JOHNNY

I CAN'T BELIEVE I almost lost all this. When you have hit rock bottom and finally climb out of the hole you've been in, you have a whole new appreciation for life. I was in the army when an IED killed my best friend and mangled my leg. I was honorably discharged from the army and for a while I lost my way in life. I got heavily into drugs, even stealing from Sierra, my late best friend's little sister. I'm not proud of it. Honestly, I'm embarrassed of everything I did. I had no family. Well, no family but Sierra. She and her husband saved me, though. They got me into rehab. Really, if I didn't go, I think Ryder would have just killed me for how much I hurt his wife. But I did it. I got clean. That was over seven years ago and I haven't touched anything since. Hell, now I hate to even take an aspirin.

Now, Ryder and Sierra have Ellie. She is a six-year-old beauty that has her 'Uncle Johnny' wrapped around her finger. Looking over at her as she comes down the slide, I can't think how thankful I am that Ryder forced me into rehab. I wouldn't give up a minute of the life I have now. I have a family now: Ryder, Sierra and Ellie.

I still haven't dated. At first, I wanted to make sure I would be able to stay clean. Then when I thought I was ready to start dating again, I decided no one would want to see the mangled thigh and leg I have. Hell, I can barely look at it.

Ellie and another little girl with bright red pigtails come running up to me, screaming, "Uncle Johnny! Uncle Johnny! Can Faith eat with us?"

I can't stop the smile that spreads across my face. Ellie knows I never tell her no. "Of course, as long as her mom and dad say it's okay."

Faith shyly points over to a man standing at the corner of the park. She mumbles to me, "My dad won't care. He's busy meeting a friend."

The man she pointed at is talking to someone and my military training puts me on high alert. Watching, I see him pass something off to the other man before I turn my attention back to the girls.

I push the happy meal I had bought myself over to her. "So Faith, what does your dad do?"

"He's a policeman." She opens up her box of food and her eyes go wide and excited. "Hey! You got a girl toy."

Chuckling at her excitement, I explain to her, "Yep. I usually get a girl toy for Ellie. But I'm sure she will be okay with you having that one."

Ellie's nodding her head as she takes a bite of her chicken nuggets. Faith opens the toy and holds the little doll in her hands, pressing it to her chest. "Thank you," she tells me happily.

Ellie nudges Faith with her elbow. "Tell him, Faith. I told you he can fix anything."

I watch her as her hands tighten on her doll and she looks at me worriedly. Her eyes immediately start to tear up and I think *oh, no*. I can handle anything but a girl crying. Hell, I have taken down six men in a bar fight, I've killed the enemy overseas without batting an eye. But a little girl crying – I can't handle that. "What is it, honey? We can fix it, but don't cry. Okay?"

She takes a deep breath and pulls her shoulders back. Right then I know this little girl is tougher than she looks. "I don't want to go with my daddy anymore."

My hands go still on the picnic table. There are so many thoughts going through my head. Does she not want to go with him because he's told her no on something? Or she misses her mommy? Or has he done something really bad to her?

I try to keep calm to get more details. I steal one of her French fries. "So, why don't you want to go with your daddy?"

She starts rubbing her shoulder and her upper arm. "He's not nice to me."

"Why do you think he's not nice to you?" I try not to scare her, but I'm holding my breath waiting for her response.

She pulls her sleeve up, showing me her arm and shoulder. "He hurt me."

She has a bright red bruise on her. It looks like a handprint. I pull out my phone and text Ryder. He and Sierra are at a doctor's appointment, which is why I have Ellie at the park. I glance over at Ellie and she's looking at her friend worriedly. I start punching in the text.

Come to the park. Now. Ellie's fine but need you here ASAP.

I hate to send it but I don't really have a choice. I have a feeling things are about to get ugly and I need him here for Ellie. At second thought, I send another text to him.

Call police.

I know he is going to be freaking out, but he also knows that I will protect Ellie at all cost.

A second goes by, and I get a response. *On my way brother.*

"Faith, what about your mommy? Where is she?"

Her face lights up. "My mommy is home."

I look over at her dad in the corner of the park and he's still talking to the same man. "Do you know your mommy's number?"

"Yes, I learned it last year." She recites it for me.

I punch it into my phone and get up from the table and walk three feet away. I'm not willing to go any further than that. "Okay, girls, finish eating. I'm going to be right here."

I hit send on my phone and wait for her mom to answer. "Hello?"

"Hello. Is this Faith's mom?"

"Yes. Oh God, is she okay? Who is this?" she asks frantically.

"My name is Johnny. I am Ellie's uncle."

I can hear her release the breath she's been holding. "Ellie from class? Okay. Is everything okay?"

"I am here at the park on 2nd and Main. Faith has asked me to not let her go with her dad. She has bruises on her..."

I can hear a door slam and then the starting of a car. "Please, please, Mister Johnny, please don't let him take her. I'm on my way."

The desperation in her voice makes me almost violent. I didn't know if she knew her daughter was being abused or not, so to hear that in her voice calms me a little. At least the little girl has someone on her side.

I hang up the phone and walk over to the girls. They both are quiet and subdued. "Okay, girls. I need you to promise me something." They both nod their heads at me. "I need you to promise that no matter what happens, you stay right here. Ellie, your daddy is on his way and when he gets here, you take Faith and go straight to him. Okay?"

Both of them are looking up at me with their eyes wide and I hate to think about what they are about to see.

"Okay, Uncle Johnny. I promise." Ellie smiles at me.

Faith looks more shook up but she nods. It makes me hate to think what all she's been through.

2

JOHNNY

When I look up, Faith's dad is walking toward us. I start walking to meet him halfway and get some distance between us and the girls.

I stop in front of him and try to block him from seeing them. "So, I've seen the bruises on her arm. I can't let you take her. I've called the police." And thankfully, the police sirens can be heard in the distance.

The rage in the other man's eyes is evil. I've seen it before. When you are over enemy lines on the battlefield, you see that hatred and pure evil then too.

"Who the fuck do you think you are? I am the cops." He shoves me to try and get by, but I don't budge.

"You are not leaving here with her. It will be over my dead body." I keep my voice calm. I learned that skill long ago. No matter what I feel, I can always control my voice.

"If that's the way you want it." He pulls a gun from his holster and points it at me. "Now, I suggest you mind your own business and let me get my daughter."

When the other park patrons see the gun, all hell breaks loose. People are screaming and running, giving me the perfect opportunity to knock the gun out of his hands, lock onto him and wrestle him to the ground.

He's grunting in pain, but I don't let up. My knee is in his back and I press harder when I look over to check on the girls, who are both crying their eyes out. But they are both sitting there, holding on to each other in the same place I left them.

I breathe a sigh of relief when I see Ryder and Sierra running toward us and then shortly after, the police are swarming the park. Even though the police are screaming freeze, Ryder doesn't stop until he gets to Ellie and Faith.

I put my hands up with my knee still in Faith's dad's

back. A policeman comes and jerks me up by the arms, then puts handcuffs on me. I don't struggle. Now that the girls are safe, I can handle whatever.

"I'm a policeman. I'm officer Caleb Johnson. This man attacked me." Faith's father is holding up his badge, hollering as he gets up from the ground.

The man holding me jerks the cuffs even tighter on my wrists. Ryder walks up to us and thankfully he recognizes most of the cops standing around. "Hey, hold on, let him go," he says. "This is my brother and he works for me. There has to be a reason for this."

I give him a nod of thanks and then look over at the girls. They are both sitting on the tabletop and Sierra has her arms around them. "I was here with my niece. Her friend joined us and asked me not to let her go with her dad. She showed me bruises on her arms and so I texted Ryder to call the police and I tried to detain him until you got here."

"Yeah, and he pulled a gun on him in a park full of kids," a man hollers twenty feet away from us. "I saw it all. I was watching him. He was doing some kind of drug deal before all that."

Caleb starts arguing, saying it's a lie and that I

attacked him. Another policeman pulls him to the edge of the park so he can cool off.

The man holding me tells his partner to go check on the girl. I stand there and watch as he approaches Faith, Ellie and Sierra. Faith starts screaming when he gets close and jumps off the table, running over to me. She grabs onto my legs, sobbing uncontrollably. "Please, don't let them take me. Please."

I start to crouch down but the policeman stops me. I turn to him and plead, "Just let me calm her down."

He nods his head and I squat down. When I do, she wraps her arms around my neck. My hands are still handcuffed behind me, but that doesn't stop me from resting my head against hers and giving her some comfort. "Honey, nobody is going to take you," I say in a soothing voice. "They just want to see your arm."

She starts sniffing, trying to get control of herself.

"Faith, Faith..." a woman is frantically screaming when she pushes past a policeman and runs toward us. The little girl in my arms doesn't let go, but she does wave and call to her mom.

She is beautiful. Her long red hair is flowing behind her. She has on a jean jacket and a green dress that shows off her legs. Her face is taut and I can see the stress and worry in her expression from here. As she gets closer, her bright green eyes are shimmering, and my first instinct is to wrap her in my arms and get her and her daughter out of here. But I can't. My wrists are still cuffed behind my back.

When she stops next to us, I see the curiosity on her face as she looks between me and her daughter, but Faith jumps into her arms. Once she's hugged her mom, she reaches around and clenches her little hand onto my shirt, with her happy meal toy in her other hand.

I want to hold her in my arms when I ask her, but I can't. "Faith, honey, I need you to show the police officer your arm."

When she starts to shake her head, I tell her, "Trust me, honey. I promise you, I will not let you go with your daddy. But you have to tell this police officer what you told me about your arm."

Her mom softens at my words and I see the look of hope in her face. My God, what have these two been through?

Faith starts sniffling and her eyes tear up, but she takes a deep breath and pulls her shirt sleeve up showing us her arm. She mumbles, "My dad is mean to me. He hurt my arm and makes me go with him to mean people's houses. I don't want to go with him anymore."

When she finishes, she dives back onto my chest and her arms go around my neck.

"You're okay, honey," I murmur to her. "You did good. I'm proud of you."

She nuzzles her face into my neck and I feel her tears soaking the collar of my shirt. The cop standing behind me undoes the cuffs and my arms instantly go around her. Her mom stands back with her hand over her mouth. She's alarmed at the connection her daughter feels toward me, and to be honest, I'm a little shaken too. But in this moment, I know that I will do everything in my power to protect her.

A police officer walks toward me. "There are about a dozen witness corroborating your story. Do you plan on filing a complaint, Mr....?"

"John Ellis. And yes, I do. So does the girl's mother." I nod over to her assuredly.

"Not that it will do any good. You do know he is a police officer, right?" she asks the cop.

He nods and I can see the disgust in his eyes. "I see

that you have had complaints before, ma'am. But we are not in his jurisdiction. He will be arrested. I can't guarantee how long he will be in, but I do promise we will pursue this. I won't stand by while someone hurts a child. An officer will be over shortly to take all the information."

3

OLIVIA

I GIVE my statement and so does Johnny. My daughter is still wrapped around his neck. I tried to pry her off, but when she protested, he assured me she was fine.

Once everything has settled down and Ryder, Sierra and Ellie leave, it's only me, Johnny, Faith and a few policeman still lingering around.

"Johnny, I don't even know what to say. I can't thank you enough for what you did for my daughter. Caleb is a bad man and I hope this doesn't affect you in any way."

"Don't worry about me. I'm fine. And I keep my promises. I won't let her go with him again."

I smile at him. He's cocky and self assured, but I

know Caleb. I know how powerful he is. The one time he hit me, I left him. But I have paid for it ever since. He never put his hands on Faith... not until today. He hasn't touched me again, but he terrorizes us. He's always had the law on his side. Which is why I had to let her go with him today. Right now, I'm saving money to run away. After all this, I might have to do that sooner rather than later.

I look over at Johnny standing with his arms still around Faith as he rubs her back. I think she's asleep, but she still hasn't loosened her hold on him. When I first ran into the park, I have to admit I was already freaked out and seeing Faith clinging to this huge man with tattoos up and down his arms scared me. But as soon as I saw him with her, how he held her protectively, I knew then that she was fine.

He smiles at me as I keep watching them. He's a big, tattooed man that looks really intimidating, but I'm beginning to think he's just a big teddy bear. My lower belly tightens. If I was interested in dating, I would love to go out with him. Too bad I'm not. Nobody wants to deal with the mess I have going on right now.

"Do you care to carry her to my car?"

He lifts her higher into his arms. "Sure. Lead the way."

He follows behind me and I can feel his eyes on me the whole way. I try not to do an extra shake of my hips, but I know it's inevitable. Any sane woman would do the same with him behind them.

I open the back door and he sets her in the seat and belts her in. When he stands up, he looks at me worriedly. "What about when she wakes up? She's going to think I left her."

My hand goes to his shoulder to reassure him. "She will be fine. I will tell her."

He nods and pulls out his wallet. Handing me his business card, he tells me, "Please, call me if you need anything."

I take it and thank him again for helping Faith. I reach up on my tiptoes and hug him. I stand there absorbing the strength and heat of his body before I step back. Blushing now, I walk around to the driver's side and drive off without looking back.

Faith was fine until I tried to carry her into the house. She woke up crying and cried most of the night. She slept with me in the bed. It was a lot for a six-year-old to go through. I didn't make her go to school the next day. I just couldn't. She was exhausted.

Sierra called midmorning to check on me and Faith. "Sierra, I'm so sorry to have involved your family in this..."

"Don't you dare apologize. You have nothing to apologize for. I had no idea what you had been going through. But now that I do, we are going to help. Ryder and Johnny already have an investigator on it."

I start to protest loudly and then realize that Faith has finally fallen asleep, so I start to whisper-yell at her. "No. Sierra. No. I can't afford that. Please..."

"You are not paying for it. Don't worry about it. Johnny is taking care of it all. What are you whispering for? Are you okay?'

I sigh, and then decide to tell her the truth. "Faith didn't sleep at all. She was up crying all night. She thinks that one of Caleb's men is going to come and take her away."

Sitting down on the couch, I lean over and put my head on my hand. It's been a long night and I don't know how much more I can take. "And what can I do, Sierra? A part of me realizes that her nightmare is something that could actually happen. I will fight with every breath in me, but how can I protect her?" Once I get it all out, I can't stop the sobbing.

"Olivia, stop. Right now, stop. Do you know how strong you are? You are one of the strongest women I know. Look how far you've already come. You can do this. And we are going to help you. Johnny is going to help you."

I don't want to ask, but I can't stop myself. "But why? Why does he want to help us?"

She laughs. "You have to know Johnny. That's just the way he is. Did you not see how Faith attached herself to him? She knows he will keep her safe."

I think back to the night before. "Yes, she is definitely attached to him. She cried for him all last night. Your daughter is lucky to have him as an uncle."

She sighs, and then tells me the full story about Johnny. About him being her late brother's best friend. His service in the army, and even his stint in rehab.

"Honestly, Olivia, he should be the one to tell you all of this, but I want you to know because I don't want you to hurt him. He's been through a lot. And if he's into Faith... and you like I think he is, then I don't want to see him get hurt."

It amazes me that she thinks I could hurt him. Yes, I'm surprised about his past, but it doesn't make him less of a man. He saved my daughter. There's no way I could look at him less after that.

I hang up after I get the pep talk and sermon from Sierra. She did make me feel better. I am better prepared to protect Faith. I have my gun permit and since I left Caleb, I carry it everywhere now. I have to defend my daughter. There is no other option.

"Mommy!" Faith screams and I run up the stairs to her. I had hoped she would sleep longer.

Johnny

MY PHONE RINGS and I look at the caller id and see it's Sierra. With a smile on my face, I answer. "Hey, sis!"

She doesn't beat around the bush. "Hey, Johnny. I need a favor."

"Sure. Anything." I stand up from my desk and stretch my arms up over my head. I have been sitting for too long.

"Can you go check on Faith and Olivia?" she asks me.

I grab my keys off the desk and start walking toward my truck. "Yes. Are they okay?"

In one quick breath, she tells me. "Well, I just got off the phone with Olivia. She's so tough, Johnny, but she doesn't know how she's going to protect Faith. And then Faith was up crying all night. I just think she needs someone right now, and Ryder won't let me go over without him and he can't get here for another hour."

I flip my phone over to the speakers on my truck. Putting it in drive, I tell Sierra not to worry. I'm on my way there now. I don't even need the address. From all my research today, I committed it to memory. I promise Sierra I will let her know later how it's going and hang up.

Pulling into Olivia's driveway, I notice an unmarked police car sitting in the front of her house. I look at the man briefly and he doesn't take his eyes off me. I walk over to him and ask him what is he doing outside my friend's house.

"I was told to watch the house," he answers simply.

Putting my hands on the door, I lean down to look

him in the eye. "Are you watching the house or the people in it?"

He only shrugs at me.

"Who asked you to do this?" I know it isn't one of our guys so all I can assume is it is one of her ex-husband's men.

When he doesn't respond, I leave him and walk up her front porch.

I knock on her front door, then look back at the car and the man is still watching me.

"Who is it?" she hollers through the door.

"Johnny." And no sooner do I get that out than the door swings open and a little redheaded girl jumps into my arms, about knocking me backwards.

"Faith! Oh my God, I'm so sorry," Olivia apologizes to me.

I hold on to her and push my way into the house past Olivia and shut and lock the door behind me.

"Hey, Faith. How you doing, honey? I hear you didn't sleep good last night." I sit down on the couch and put her on my knee.

She just shakes her head side to side.

"Well, that's okay. I'm here now, so how about we sit here and watch a little television?"

She says okay and hands me the remote, then sits next to me on the couch. Olivia is just staring at the two of us like she can't figure out what is happening. I smile at her to try and reassure her, but I don't think it's helping. Exhaustion is evident on her face, and it kills me to see her like this. I no sooner get a family movie on than Faith is leaning into me, yawning.

Once I feel her body go limp against me, I reach over to Olivia to get her attention. She startles, like she was in a trance. I would say she needs some sleep as well.

"Honey, I don't want to scare you, but there is a man sitting outside of your house," I tell her calmly.

She shrugs matter-of-factly. "Yeah, I know. He's the one that Caleb always has watching and following us. He's the reason that Faith is scared to go to school, afraid to go out in the yard and play... she's just afraid all the time."

I can't stand to hear the defeat in her voice. It kills me. I pull away from Faith and lay her down on the cushions where I was sitting. When I see that she is going to stay asleep, I walk over to Olivia and pull her up from the chair. Sitting down, I pull her down into my lap.

She struggles against me but my arms go tighter around her. "Olivia, stop," I beg her. "You're so tired, honey. Just let me hold you."

"I'm too big to sit on your lap," she tells me and looks away from me with her face red.

I pull her chin toward me so she has to meet my eyes. "Have you looked at me?"

She looks at me with confusion.

"I'm huge. You are tiny compared to me. You are definitely not too big to hold," I assure her and lean back, pulling her with me.

My arms are around her and she lies stiffly against me. I try to get her mind off of it and decide right then that I'm going to take control of the situation.

"I know you don't know me. You probably don't trust me..." I start.

She interrupts. "I trust you. How could I not after last night? He held a gun to you... and you protected my daughter."

Good. Well, that is one thing less to worry about.

And I tell her so. "I am going to take you and Faith out of town for a while. My friend has a lake house and we are going to go there for a few days. We will be back for the court date on Monday."

She looks startled. "Court date? What court date?"

I stroke my hand up and down her back and I can't help but appreciate her curves being pressed into me. I can feel my cock harden underneath her but I try to focus on her question. "I got the hearing pushed through quicker. They are going to do a temporary custody hearing. You and Faith are not going to be able to work or go to school this week. Not with him outside and following you. It's only three days she will miss from school. Just time for me to get you away to protect you and then Ryder can stay here and take care of the investigation."

She looks at me with hope in her eyes and then just as quickly it's gone. "I can't miss that much work.. the money."

Frustrated, I tell her, "Forget about the money. Look at her, honey." I point over to Faith. Even in her sleep you can see her swollen eyes and lips from all the crying. "Let me take care of you both. She needs this. You need this."

I can see her mind going a mile a minute. When I'm absolutely positive she is about to tell me no, she nods her head okay.

I lean in and kiss her forehead. "Okay, let's pack and get things ready."

4

OLIVIA

We had to sneak out of my house. Johnny left out the front door and drove away, circling to the neighborhood behind us. Faith and I wheeled a bag out the back door and through the neighbors' yard. As Johnny loaded up our bags, I helped Faith get into the truck. We went by his house so he could grab some clothes.

Now we are driving down the highway and for the first time in a long time, I feel safe. I can't think about how much this life I chose is going to mess up Faith. She seems to be doing better now that Johnny is with is. When I look over at him, he smiles, calming me too.

My mind keeps going back to earlier sitting on his lap and letting him hold me. He's right. He is massive. I found myself curling into him and resting my head on his shoulder while he stroked my back. I tried to ignore his hardness underneath me. Neither one of us mentioned it, but probably both of us knew it wasn't the right time. I know it's crazy that I'm going off with this man that I met less than 24 hours ago. But just like I told him… I trust him.

A few hours go by and Faith has already fallen asleep again. She really was tired. We pull up to a beautiful house sitting on the shores of a lake. I get out to grab Faith, but Johnny hands me the keys to the house. "Unlock the door, honey. I'll carry in Faith and the luggage." I lead him to the front door and open it. I can't stop the gasp that escapes from my lips. It's an open room plan, and the whole back wall is windows with picturesque views of the lake. He walks into a room off to the side and I follow him. I watch as he pulls the covers back and lays Faith down on the bed, then covers her up.

When he stands up, he's looking down at her and I'm in awe of the relationship that these two have already built.

He points to a door on the other side of the room. "That is the bathroom and it also adjoins to your bedroom. My room is on the other side of the living room. Get comfy. I'm going to go grab the bags."

I watch him walk out of the room and have to stop myself from following him. The safety I feel when I'm with him makes me want to be with him always.

Johnny

I WALK OUT to the truck and try to catch my bearings. I send a text to Sierra and Ryder to let them know what's up. I then open the door to grab a few things and the smell of her, that damn fresh coconut and vanilla scent that I breathed in the whole way here, hits my nostrils and I take a deep breath. My cock has been hard since I had her in my lap at her house. Sitting next to her in the truck for the few hours it took to get here was pure torture. I don't know how I'm going to keep my hands off of her, but I do know my number one priority is to keep them both safe. They both need some normalcy in their lives right now.

When I go back in the house, I peek in on Faith and see that she is still sleeping. The water is running in the bathroom and images of Olivia standing under the spray go through my head. Fuck! I back out of the little girl's room and go over to Olivia's, putting her suitcase on the bed. As I turn to leave, Olivia walks out of the bathroom wrapped only in a towel. Her hair is in a knot on the top of her head and the towel barely reaches her thigh. I can't do anything but stand there and stare at her.

When my gaze goes back up to her face, I register the shock in her eyes. She's staring straight at the bulge in my pants. "I'm so sorry. Uh, there's your bag. I'll leave you to it."

I stride out of there, grab my bag and slam the door to my room. Fuck, I'm not going to make it. She is perfection. She is crazy if she thinks she is too big. My mouth waters just thinking about her standing there with a towel barely covering her magnificent curves. I grip onto my length and shift around to try and get more comfortable. I count to 100 and try to think of anything but her to try and get my erection to go down. As a last resort, I go into the bathroom to take a cold shower.

Once I'm out and dressed, I hear the doorbell ring. I had Olivia order food delivery from a local grocery on the way here. It must be them.

After tipping the grocer deliverer, I'm unpacking the

bags, and Olivia walks in to help. She is blushing still and I can't help but think how cute she is with her red cheeks and red hair.

I keep unpacking bags and know that I have to tell her. "I'm sorry about earlier. I should have knocked or something." I put the eggs and milk in the refrigerator and then turn to her. "I'm not going to lie to you, Olivia. I'm attracted to you – which I'm guessing you probably already realized. But I want you to know that I don't plan on taking advantage of this situation. Maybe when we get through this, I can take you out on a date if you want to?"

She's looking at me and I can tell she's trying to get the nerve up to say something. What it is I don't know. Is she going to tell my tattoo-covered ass to take a leap? Say thank you, but no? I don't know, but I do know I'm holding my breath waiting on her to say something.

She walks over to me and doesn't stop until I can feel the roundness of her breasts pressed against my chest. I suck in a breath at the contact.

Her hand wraps around my neck and pulls me down to her. "I want you, Johnny. I don't want to wait. I know we are in a mess right now. But I also know you are a good man. You wouldn't be taking advantage of me, because I want you too."

She seals her lips over mine. My arms go around her and pull her even tighter against me. I ravage her lips but still I feel like I can't get close enough to her. Her mouth opens under mine and I plunge my tongue into its depths until I'm pulling away from her, gasping for breath. Her lips are swollen and her eyes are hooded.

I take a deep breath and let it out. I'm still holding her in my arms, because I need to be honest with her, but I have to hold her. "Honey, God, I want this. I want this more than you know. But you have to know I'm not a good man."

She laughs. Literally laughs in my face. "I know we just met, but you do remember saving my daughter, right? In my book, that makes you a good man... the best man."

I can't stop the smile on my face, but quickly respond. "But there are things you don't know about me. I'm a recovering addict..."

"Yeah, that's been clean for seven years. I know. Sierra told me when she was warning me not to hurt you." She tries to pull me back down to her.

I can't resist and lean down to kiss her and then pull away. "She warned you not to hurt me?"

She's laughing again. "Yeah, I know it's crazy... like I could hurt you."

I press her hand to my heart. I know she feels the thud, thud, thud through my shirt. It's about to explode from my chest. "Honey, you could probably break me."

"Johhhnnnnyyy! Mommmmy!" Faith yells from the other room.

I kiss Olivia on the cheek and tell her we'll talk about this later. Pulling away from her, I catch Faith in my arms as she catapults herself to me when she runs into the kitchen.

5

OLIVIA

Hours later, I'm laying in Faith's bed until she falls asleep. I can't help but think about Johnny and Faith. He spent the whole afternoon entertaining and playing with her. She is super smart for a six-year-old but these last few weeks have caused her to regress in her behavior, making her extra needy.

By the end of the night, thank goodness, I was seeing more signs of her old self. Johnny was very patient with her and gave her time to get accustomed to her new surroundings before gently pushing her to be more independent. She blossomed under his praise and if possible, I wanted him even more.

"Mom, what are we doing tomorrow?" Faith asks me groggily, interrupting my thoughts.

"I think we are going to the lake for the day. Go to sleep, honey."

She yawns loudly and lays her head back down on the pillow.

I lay there until I am sure she is asleep and hear her slight snoring. I get up and walk into the adjoining bathroom. Looking in the mirror, I inspect my face and think that I look way older than my twenty-five years. Staring at myself, I can't help but question the decision I know I'm about to make. I want Johnny. There is no doubt about it. He doesn't think he's a good man, but I know the truth. I know only a good man would treat Faith and me the way he is treating us.

Stripping down to my bra and panties, I can't help but look at my wide hips and heavy breasts, which never perked back up after giving birth. And then there are the marks on my belly. I can't say I hate them. I don't like them, but they are there because of Faith, and I wouldn't change that for anything. Walking into my bedroom, I pull a T-shirt out of my suitcase, put it on and go into the living room.

Johnny is lying on the couch with the TV on low and his feet up on the table. He doesn't move, so I assume he's sleeping. I walk over to him, just because I want a better look. His arms and chest are covered in tattoos. He looks so peaceful. When I get to the couch, I sit down next to him softly. My hand inches across his chest and when I barely touch him, his hand reaches out and grabs mine.

"Honey, are you trying to sneak up on me?" He pulls me until I'm lying across him.

I lay my head down and put a brief kiss on his chest. "No, I was just wanting a better look, that's all." I trace one of the letters with my finger.

"You can look all you want. But I think we need to wait on everything else," he says as he brushes the hair off my face.

I try to pull back from him, but he grips my arms and holds me still. "What are you thinking? Why are you frowning?"

I stubbornly sit up and move away from him. "Nothing. No reason. I thought we uh, well... if you aren't interested, I'm not going to beg for it."

He sits up and moves over next to me. "Look at me." When I don't respond, he puts a hand under my chin and pulls it his way. "Look at me, honey. I do want you. There's no doubt about that. I've been hard since the first time I saw you. But you have so much going on. I saw you today. You are so worried about losing your daughter... I just don't want to add to everything else you have going on. That's all."

I consider what he said, but I also know that this is what I need... he is what I need. "Do you really want me, Johnny?" I ask him shyly.

He pulls my hand between his legs and wraps our hands around his hard shaft. I squeeze a little and he moans. "Yes, I want you, Olivia."

Looking into this eyes, I see the sincerity there. I stand up and hold my hand out to him. When he puts his hand in mine, I tug him up until he's standing and then I lead him over to his room. I stop when I get to the side of the bed. Dropping his hand, I pull my T-shirt over my head.

He looks down at my body and instead of covering myself, I stand there before him, insecure, but determined to not shy away from what I want. And want I want is him.

"Fuck, baby. You're perfect." His hands go around me and unsnap by bra. He lets it fall to the floor and then cups each of my breasts in his hands. His thumbs flick across my nipples and I inhale sharply at the contact, my nipples beading at his touch.

When he touches me with his lips and sucks me into his mouth, a guttural moan escapes from his lips and I hold on to his head, keeping him there – right against me.

He puts his fingers in the waistband of my panties and pulls them down my legs. He goes down to his knees, kissing my body the lower he goes. When I step out of my underwear, he pushes me back onto the bed and slides his shoulders between my legs.

His finger traces along the seam of my folds. I'm slick, wet, and open to his caress. He traces along my opening and then moves to the swollen clit. I'm in agony as he applies pressure until I'm about to go over the edge and then he pulls back until I'm calm again. Back and forth, start and stop, I'm begging him for it. I'm not proud, but he brings this out of me. I want it... I want him inside me.

***

Johnny

SHE'S SO CLOSE. I know it wouldn't take much to put her over the edge. But I don't want to yet. When I do finally let her come, I want to be inside her. I want to feel her channel vibrating around me.

Her arousal is driving me mad and I don't even try to stop myself from putting my mouth on her, my plan of making her wait forgotten. When her taste hits my tongue, I moan against her and instantly she comes undone, exploding around me. I kiss up her body as she reaches down to undo my pants.

"Honey, wait." I roll over on my back, still trying to catch my breath and realize I should have had this discussion with her before now. "I was injured in the army. My thigh and leg is a little mangled... it's not pretty."

She rolls over onto her side with her hand drawing circles around my belly button. "I'm sorry you were hurt. But there's nothing that you could say that will make me want to stop."

She unzips my pants and tugs them down my legs. Once they're off, she touches me through my underwear. My cock is hard and oozing precum, ready for her. Like it's begging to get inside of her.

She slowly pulls them down and my cock like a slingshot bounces back up. She kisses up my body and the closer she gets to my upper leg, the more tense I get. No one has seen this except for doctors and I'm a little nervous about it. When her lips touch my mangled skin, I gasp and look down at her. She's looking at me with compassion and something else, but not pity. Thank God. Pity I couldn't take right now.

When she kisses up my thigh I tug her arms and pull her up until she's sitting astride me. My cock is pressing against her naked bottom and her gentle movements against me have me thrusting my hips up to press into her.

"Ride me, baby. It's killing me, I want to be inside you," I beg her.

She starts to lift herself and then stops. "I'm clean. I haven't been with Caleb..."

"I don't want to know about you and Caleb, honey. I don't want him in this room or in your head. I'm clean too. It's been... a long time for me." I lean up to meet her halfway and kiss her.

"I'm on the pill, too, so you don't have to worry about that either," she whispers against my lips.

"I wasn't worried about it." If she knew the thoughts that are going through my head, she would probably run out of here screaming. I don't tell her that I want to bury my seed in her womb over and over until I'm sure that she's pregnant. I don't tell her that I want to get inside her and then never let her walk away.

I do tell her, "Baby, I have to get inside you... now."

She raises up and, grasping my hard cock, she lines it up at her center. She slowly lowers herself onto me and I can feel her tight tunnel expand around me. She's hugging my cock tightly and I groan at the intense feeling of possession I feel at this moment. Her gaze is locked on mine and as she gyrates her hips and bounces up and down, I get lost in the ecstasy in her eyes. She's everything, she's perfection and I grab tightly on to her hips, thrusting up inside her. Her face shows every emotion: pain when I dig my hands into her hips, elation with each thrust. When all you can hear in the room is our ragged breathing and the slapping of our sweaty bodies, I get lost in her and tell her to come. "Come for me, baby. Give it all to me."

As if on command, she moans out my name and her pussy clenches tightly to me. "Yes, Johnny. Yes. Don't stop."

"Never. Never, honey." I give her a final thrust and stay there until I feel our juices coming out of her, coating my balls and my stomach.

When she raises off of me and tries to get off the bed, I tug her arm.

"Where do you think you're going?" I ask her between kisses. I swear even though I was just inside her, it wasn't enough.

"I was going to get cleaned up," she tells me, laughingly.

I tweak her nipple until she moans. "Well, I like you dirty."

She nibbles on my neck and ear and whispers, "I bet you do, Johnny."

6

OLIVIA

THE FEW DAYS at the lake house have flown by. He has spent every minute of every day with us. He gives me breaks and sends me off to read or take a bath while he watches Faith. He dotes on her and totes her around. I've never seen her so happy and carefree.

It's always on the edge of my mind that I might possibly lose her. God, I hope not. There's been so many times that I thought I should just pack up and run. Run so that Caleb will never find us.

I confided that to Johnny last night, but all he would tell me is that I can't run anywhere without him and that I needed to trust him. He assured me that Ryder is working on something against Caleb and he promises me that there is no way he will ever let Caleb take Faith again. I want to trust him. I want to believe him. But there's always a shadow over us just because of the uncertainty. The uncertainty of everything.

The hearing is tomorrow at 1 p.m. We thought about going back tonight, but none of us were ready to leave so we decided to wait until morning. We tried to explain to Faith what she would have to do tomorrow, and told her that all she had to do was tell the truth. She was really nervous about it until Johnny told her that he would be right by her side the whole time. He's promised her over and over that she would not have to go with her dad. God, I hope he can keep that promise.

We finally got Faith asleep and tonight, Johnny is sleeping in my room. We've been together every night since the first night. Each night I stay longer and longer, until finally I was sneaking out of the room right before Faith woke up.

He's holding me in his arms and there is no other place that I want to be. His hand is stroking my back and my hand is laying on his chest. I'm sad, really. Sad that this is about to end and we have to go back to real life. Sad that I don't know what tomorrow holds and sad that I don't know what Johnny's thinking. He did everything to reassure Faith, but I can tell he is stressed out. He spent quite a bit of time on the phone this afternoon, but when I asked him, he didn't want to talk about it. God, I hope everything works out.

Johnny

I SPENT the whole night holding Olivia in my arms. I faded in and out of sleep until the sun started peeking through the blinds. I start packing, waiting until the very last minute to wake the girls up. I know neither one of them slept well.

When I start loading the car, Olivia comes out to help. She hands me her suitcase. "Sorry I slept late."

I kiss her lips and see the tiredness in her eyes. "It's okay, honey. You needed it."

She smiles at me, but it doesn't reach her eyes. I grip the suitcase in my hand tighter because I hate to see her like this.

"I missed you this morning," she whispers against my lips.

I lace my fingers around hers and walk with her back to the house. "I missed you too. I'm not going to keep sneaking out of your room. After everything settles down, we are going to sit down and talk."

She looks at me with confusion, but doesn't ask me anything.

When we finally get on the road, Olivia and Faith are both a basket of nerves. I try to make them laugh, even singing to them off key with the radio.

Going straight to the court house, we walk into the room with Olivia's hand in mine and Faith on my hip.

We sit and wait our turn and when Olivia's name is called she walks to the front. I have Faith sitting beside me but I hate that I can't go up there with her.

Caleb comes in a few minutes late looking like he doesn't have a care in the world. He smirks at Olivia and my fist clenches, wanting to go and punch that smirk off his face.

Ryder is supposed to be here, but he must be running

late. I get a vibration in my pocket and pull my phone out. It's a text from Ryder.

I'm on my way. I have good news.

Sighing in relief, I text him back. *Hurry*

The judge comes in and everyone stands. He goes over the proceedings and what happened at the incident. Today's hearing is a temporary custody hearing and he is stressing that he is going to do what is best for the child.

He listens to the case, the testimony of a few witnesses and then when we think he is about to make the judgment, he asks if Faith is in the room. Her mom says yes and both Faith and I stand. When the judge asks for Faith to join him in his chambers, she grabs my hand and we walk toward him.

The judge stops us. "Alone. I would like to talk to her alone."

"Sir, no disrespect, but where she goes, I go. My name is Johnny Ellis. I have been hired as her bodyguard and as an advocate for the child. The papers were filed this morning."

He looks over at the court reporter, who is going

through her papers. When she nods her head at him, he tells me, "Okay, let's go."

We walk out of the room as her father hollers that he objects. Thankfully, the judge is not listening to it.

Faith never lets go of my hand. She tells the judge exactly how she feels about her dad and everything he has put her through. She even tells him about his friends following her everywhere and not being able to go out and play.

The judge thanks her and then dismisses us. I smile at Olivia when we come out to try and reassure her, but she looks beyond stressed out. When the judge walks back to the courtroom, he no sooner sits down than a woman walks in and hands him a piece of paper. Faith and I go back and sit down and Ryder is there waiting for us. He gives me a thumbs-up and I'm praying that he worked it out.

The judge then begins to speak. "After everything that I have heard today, in the best interests of the child, I am placing her in the temporary custody of her mother, Olivia Johnson, until the hearing, which is set for one month from today. It is not common that you see such a disregard of the law or abuse of power, especially from someone that is supposed to be a man of the law. I make this ruling also because I have been asked to detain Mr. Caleb Johnson." He pauses and gestures for the bailiff to come forward. "Mr. Caleb Johnson is under arrest for drug distribution, trafficking and human trafficking. Mrs. Johnson, you and Faith are free to go. And can I add you should be very proud of that girl. Hearing adjourned."

By this point, Caleb is hollering and struggling against the court officer. But I ignore all of that, I pick up Faith and we rush over to where Olivia is standing with her mouth wide open, and tears streaming down her face.

She kisses Faith and then me. "You did it. I can't believe you did it."

I wish I could take all the credit, but I can't. I point over at Ryder. "Actually, he did it." I hug him and slap him on the back. "I owe you, brother."

He shrugs his shoulders, shaking off Olivia's thank yous.

When we walk out of the court house, I can't take my eyes off of my girls. Both of their faces are beaming and I'm so happy that it all worked out.

Pulling Olivia's hand up to my lips, I kiss her palm. "Well, I know one of the first things we need to take care of." She's smiling ear to ear as I continue. "I hated hearing them call you Mrs. Johnson. I think we need to change that."

Her eyes widen in shock, but I still see the hope there.

EPILOGUE

OLIVIA

A Few Weeks Later

AFTER THE HEARING, everything seemed to go back to normal. Faith went back to her confident, sassy self and I went back to work. The only difference is that we spend every bit of our spare time with Johnny. He kept his promise. He protected us and continues to do so.

We just finished eating dinner and Faith is in the living room watching TV. Johnny and I are washing dishes and he's been quiet the whole night, like he has something on his mind.

Finally fed up, I drop the pan into the soapy water and it splashes all over the both of us. Now that I have his attention, I tell him, "Just say it. Tell me whatever it is that's bothering you." God, I hope he's not breaking up with me. Everything has been so perfect.

He pulls me against him and stares into my eyes. He's not smiling, and he's making me nervous. "Honey, I'm tired of sneaking out early in the morning. I'm tired of hiding what we have from Faith. I love you. I love both of you and I want you to be my wife. If you're not ready..."

Sobbing, I hold on to him. "I'm ready. There's nothing I would want more than to be your wife."

"So will you be my daddy?" a quiet voice asks me from the doorway.

Johnny and I gasp and look at Faith. My hands clench at my heart. My little girl has been through so much. Her dad is still in jail and he will not be getting out anytime soon. She is so attached to Johnny and I know she would love to have him for a Dad. Johnny walks over to her and squats down in front of her. "Yes. I would be your step dad."

She considers what he said and then asks him, "Can I call you Dad?"

He wipes at his eyes and then huskily whispers to her, "Yes, honey. I would love for you to call me

Dad." He gets a jewelry box out of his back pocket and opens it to show her. "I have a ring for your mommy, but I wanted to get you something too. To let you know that I love you and I will always be here for you."

"Do you promise?" she asks with so much hope in her eyes it about kills me. I'm steadily wiping the tears out of my eyes.

"I promise," he pledges to her. He helps her put the necklace on and when we both praise how beautiful she looks, she walks back into the living room. When he turns to me, he still has tears in his eyes.

Pulling another box out of his pocket, he opens it to show me the ring. "I love you, honey." And he puts his ring on my finger with a promise of forever.

JOIN ME!

JOIN MY NEWSLETTER & READERS GROUP

For Up To Date Information on New Releases, Specials, and More

www.AuthorHopeFord.com/subscribe

https://www.facebook.com/groups/hopeford/

A place to talk about Hope Ford's books! Find out about new releases, giveaways, get exclusive content, see covers before anyone else and more!

Find Hope Ford at www.authorhopeford.com

ABOUT THE AUTHOR

Bestselling short romance author Hope Ford writes short, steamy, sweet romances. She loves tattooed, alpha men, instant love stories, and ALWAYS happily ever afters. She has over 70 books and they are all available on Amazon.

Follow Hope Ford on Pinterest, Instagram, Facebook, Goodreads, and more!

www.AuthorHopeFord.com/Follow-Me

Printed in Great Britain
by Amazon